"Let's dance."

Liz felt a spurt of adrenaline as Connor pulled her into his arms and drew her close to his hard-muscled body. His hat nudged hers, but he didn't let that stop him from pressing his cheek against hers. She was burning up. He couldn't help but notice.

When the song ended, he didn't let go. "This is nice," he whispered in a husky voice.

So nice she could hardly breathe. He continued to rock her in his arms until another song began. "I like your gold barrel-racer earrings. They're unique."

Liz lost track of her surroundings. The whole time they clung to each other, his warm breath tickled the ends of her newly cut hair, sending rivulets of delight through her body. It was uncanny how they moved as one person.

Dear Reader,

A Cowboy's Heart, the second book in my Hitting Rocks Cowboys series, is a story I've wanted to write for a long time. I've rarely written about two people who, because of circumstances beyond their control, were just friends all their lives. Then circumstances change and they are thrown together in a way that allows them to see beneath the surface. It's a huge risk for my heroine, who's always had a crush on the hero, but she's determined to find out if the book is even better than the gorgeous cover.

Enjoy!

Rebecca Winters

A COWBOY'S HEART

REBECCA WINTERS

HARLEQUIN® AMERICAN ROMANCE®

Recycling programs
for this product may
not exist in your area.

ISBN-13: 978-0-373-75532-5

A COWBOY'S HEART

Printed in U.S.A.

ABOUT THE AUTHOR

Rebecca Winters, whose family of four children has now swelled to include five beautiful grandchildren, lives in Salt Lake City, Utah, in the land of the Rocky Mountains. With canyons and high-alpine meadows full of wildflowers, she never runs out of places to explore. They, plus her favorite vacation spots in Europe, often end up as backgrounds for her romance novels, because writing is her passion, along with her family and church.

Rebecca loves to hear from readers. If you wish to email her, please visit her website, www.cleanromances.com.

Books by Rebecca Winters

HARLEQUIN AMERICAN ROMANCE

1261—THE CHIEF RANGER
1275—THE RANGER'S SECRET
1302 A MOTHER'S WEDDING DAY
        "A Mother's Secret"
1310—WALKER: THE RODEO LEGEND
1331—SANTA IN A STETSON
1339—THE BACHELOR RANGER
1367—RANGER DADDY
1377—A TEXAS RANGER'S CHRISTMAS
1386—THE SEAL'S PROMISE*
1398—THE MARSHAL'S PRIZE*
1422—THE TEXAS RANGER'S REWARD*
1451—THE WYOMING COWBOY**
1467—HOME TO WYOMING**
1471—HER WYOMING HERO**
1494—IN A COWBOY'S ARMS†

*Undercover Heroes
**Daddy Dude Ranch
†Hitting Rocks Cowboys

Many thanks to three remarkable ladies who were kind enough to give their time and answer some of my questions about the rodeo world:

Leslie DiMenichi with the WPRA, professional horse trainer, barrel champion rodeo competitor and breed show trainer.

Sue Smith, 2x NFR Qualifier, Circuit Finalist & Year End Winner, Calgary 100k Winner, Multiple Futurity and Derby Winner, Amateur Rodeo Barrel Racing and Breakaway Roping Winner.

Martha Josey, WPRA, AQHA and NBHA World Champion Barrel Racer, Cowgirl Hall of Fame in 1985, representing the United States in the 1988 Winter Olympics in Calgary, Canada.

Chapter One

November 28 and Mother Nature had decided to dump new snow over the Pryor Mountains on both sides of the Montana–Wyoming border. Ten inches during the night. Their biggest storm so far this year.

Liz Henson, the top barrel-racing champion in both the Montana Pro Rodeo Regional Circuit and the Dodge Ram pro finals in Oklahoma, left the barn astride Sunflower. She headed toward the covered arena behind the Hensons' small house that sat on Corkin property. With this snow she was glad she'd had the farrier in White Lodge check both her horses' shoes yesterday.

Both she and Sunflower enjoyed the invigorating air as her horse made tracks in the pristine white fluff past the Corkin ranch house. Liz's parents had worked for the Corkins since before she was born. Sadie Corkin was Liz's best friend, and both families had shared the barn over the years.

Every dawn, like clockwork, Liz got up to put her horse through a practice session before she left for work as a vet at the clinic in White Lodge twenty minutes away. Sometimes it was a trail ride, other times flat work in the arena. She tried to vary the experience for Sunflower.

Every night at dusk she went through another practice session. Barrel racing required months of progressively harder and more challenging work to build up her horse's tolerance to intense acceleration and turning. She needed to spark her horse out of some rollbacks, yet keep her soft and relaxed.

Today she wanted to work on her horse's shoulders. Mac Henson, her father, idol and mentor, had explained that the more control you had over the shoulders, the easier it would be to steer Sunflower. He'd warned Liz about everything that could happen during competition.

Her horse might be too hot and nervous, or refuse to rate or stop. It might dive into the barrel and knock it over, or misbehave in the alleyway and balk at entering the arena.

Liz had received a five-second penalty in a competition when Sunflower had dropped her shoulder at the barrel. Since then they'd been practicing correct body arc and position around the barrels.

A horse was generally left-sided, just as most humans were right-handed. The trick during the lope or canter was to shape your horse for either turn by using reverse-arc exercises and riding serpentines. She needed to teach her horse to lift the shoulder away from the pressure of the inside rein.

If the problem couldn't be mastered, she wouldn't have a prayer of winning at the Pro National Finals Rodeo in Las Vegas in December. The Mack Center on the University of Nevada campus hosted the top rodeo competitors in the world.

She might have made it to number two out of the top fifteen money winners in her event, but without constant practice and staying in excellent physical form to make her legs strong, she couldn't expect to come out with the overall win. Sadly, this would be her last competition before she gave it up to devote herself full time to her career. Dr. Rafferty needed a partner who wasn't off every few days barrel racing in another rodeo to stack up wins.

Her seven-year-old quarter horse had been a runner from the beginning and was well proportioned. Liz had trained half a dozen horses, but felt she couldn't have found a better horse for the sport than this one.

Polly, the other quarter horse Liz trained and took with her to every rodeo, wasn't as reliable as Sunflower. But if something happened to Sunflower during competition, Liz needed a backup.

Her third horse, Maisy, she left behind. She wasn't as teachable and hadn't learned to body rate or lower her head when Liz pulled on the reins. The ability for a horse to slow its speed at the first barrel in response to light rein pressure was crucial. Only then could you position it for a precise first turn and properly align it to change leads for the other two turns, thus shaving off time.

When Liz's body relaxed, Maisy should have related that to the movement. She tried to teach Maisy, but the horse was slow to respond. Nevertheless, she was a great horse for riding in the mountains.

Since Liz used dressage in her training regimen, snaffles were the best bit to use. This morning she was using training reins and had picked the square mouthpiece O-ring to teach control and collection. This bit kept her horse's mouth moist without damaging it.

Liz had about ten different bits, but didn't have a favorite competition bit. No matter which one she used, she rarely rode Sunflower in the same bit she was running and changed it frequently to keep the horse's mouth soft.

Liz trained with four barrels, arranged in what was called the cloverleaf pattern, even though there were only three for competition. Her dad had taught her that if you went for the diamond pattern, the horse wouldn't know which barrel was first, thereby reducing the excitement so her horse would stay controlled. A clever trick that worked.

Once inside the arena, Liz spent time making perfect circles with Sunflower, starting at fifty feet and diminishing to twelve, so the horse would get used to going in circles using a little inside leg. Her horse's back feet needed to go in the same track as her front feet. Liz worked Sunflower in one direction, then the other, making as many circles as necessary to get that control, sometimes walking, sometimes jogging, sometimes loping and trotting where Liz could stand in the stirrups to strengthen her legs.

Barrel racing was all about speed transitions, stops and then backing up. But Liz had learned that "all go and no whoa" wasn't fun. An effective warm-up was everything. She walked Sunflower over to the fence, stopped, backed up, then went in the other direction, using the "whoa" to alert her horse to stop. This exercise built up her horse's hindquarters. Practicing at the fence caused Sunflower to use her back hocks and stifles to turn around, building vital control.

When the moment came, Liz walked her horse along the wall, using her right hand to tip the horse's nose slightly toward the wall. She kept her left hand low and moved it out in the direction she wanted to move the shoulders.

Then she pressed the horse up by the girth with her right leg to push its shoulders away from the wall. When she felt Sunflower take two steps off her leg, she released the pressure and let the horse walk out straight.

"Good girl, Sunflower."

Liz repeated this process in the other direction, and eventually Sunflower progressed to the trot and canter stages.

The sound of clapping caused her head to jerk around.

"You're looking on top of your game, Liz."

To her surprise, it was Connor Bannock from the neighboring ranch. Coming from him there couldn't be a greater compliment. At her first junior rodeo competition years earlier, she'd blown it so badly she'd wanted to die. But Connor, who was a year older and already on his way to a world championship, had sought her out. In front of a lot of people he'd told her she had real talent and shouldn't let one loss be a reason to give up. His encouragement, plus the way he'd smiled and tipped his hat, had lit a fire in her that had never gone out.

"I'm working on it." She walked Sunflower toward him. "As usual, your fame precedes you. I just heard about your latest win. Congratulations."

"Thanks."

He and his hazer, Wade Torney, had already returned from the rodeo in Kalispell. Wade, who rode parallel to the steer as it left the chute to keep it traveling in a straight line, had been Connor's partner for years. They must have driven hard through the snow to make it back this fast.

Now the twenty-seven-year-old world steer-wrestling champion sat astride one of his stallions, wearing a shearling sheepskin jacket and his trademark cream-colored Stetson. The man was a legend.

In his teen years, Connor had been Montana's high school all-around steer wrestling and team roping champion two years in a row. Early in his career he'd stacked up dozens of awards, among them the PRCA Overall and the Steer Wrestling Resistol Rookie of the Year.

To the envy of the other competitors, last year he won his fifth world title, placing in seven out of ten rounds at the Wrangler NFR, winning the fourth round in 3.3 seconds. The list of his achievements over ten years went on and on. She knew all of them.

Beneath his cowboy hat, a pair of piercing brown eyes studied her with a thoroughness that puzzled her. Without his hat, his overly long dark-blond hair was gilded at the tips by the sun.

What was the divorced, hard-muscled rancher doing over here? Nature had played all sorts of surprises this morning. First the snow, and now the powerfully built man who'd made the cover of a dozen Western magazines naming him the sexiest cowboy of the year.

No doubt about it. The six-foot-three, two-hundred-pound bulldogger attracted a huge share of buckle bunnies who followed him around the circuit. When she was a young and impressionable teenager, the sight of him used to make Liz's heart bounce like a Ping-Pong ball.

But Liz was a twenty-six-year-old woman now,

who'd had relationships with several great guys. At the moment she was dating Kyle James, a pilot with an air charter service out of Bozeman. He'd flown in some supplies for Dr. Rafferty on an emergency. Liz had met his plane at the airfield outside White Lodge.

His good looks and friendly nature appealed to Liz. He ended up flying to White Lodge several times to take her to dinner. She'd driven to Bozeman twice to spend time with him. He was growing on her, but when he'd offered to drive with her to Las Vegas, she'd turned him down, explaining that she'd made other arrangements.

Not to be discouraged, he'd told her he planned to fly down for the last event on the fourteenth. Though she hadn't told him not to come, she wasn't sure she wanted him there. Her hesitation to let him into her life to that degree proved she wasn't ready for a full-blown relationship yet.

As Connor continued to study her, she started to grow anxious. Over the past eight years he'd only stepped on Corkin property twice that she knew of. The first time was the day of Daniel Corkin's funeral in May, when all the Bannocks showed up, except for Connor's father, Ralph, who'd been too weak to come.

The second time was the night, a month later, when Connor and his brother Jarod had rescued Sadie from their mentally unbalanced cousin, Ned Bannock. He'd trespassed on Corkin property and attacked Sadie in the barn. For the present, Ned was being treated in a special mental health facility in Billings.

Her body tautened. Connor would never have come to the ranch, especially this early, if something weren't wrong that could affect her on a personal level. "You must have bad news, otherwise you wouldn't be here. Has something happened to my father?" Her dad was the Corkin foreman and had left the house early to talk business with Zane Lawson, Sadie's stepuncle. He was the new owner of the Corkin ranch.

"If it had, do you think we'd still be here talking?"

She blinked. "But—"

"It's not your mom, either." He read her mind with ease. "This has nothing to do with your parents."

Though relieved, she bit her lip. "Then, is your father ill again? Do you need help?" Liz adored Ralph Bannock, the patriarch of the Bannock family. A great rodeo champion himself in his twenties, he'd always encouraged her and Sadie in their barrel racing. But he'd suffered a serious bout of pneumonia last spring that had put him in the hospital. Since then he'd recovered, but he was getting older and more frail. So what was *wrong?*

CONNOR WAS TAKEN aback by the questions, and the look of alarm in Liz's eyes told him how much she cared for his father. He found himself touched by her concern. "He was fine when I left him after breakfast."

"Thank goodness. When I visited with him a couple of days ago, he seemed well." She looked anxious. "What aren't you telling me?" She was really worried.

Liz was all business. It shouldn't have surprised him. She had every right to be suspicious of his unexpected presence. If it hadn't for Daniel Corkin, who'd warned the Bannocks off his property several decades ago—which meant staying away from the Hensons, too—Connor would have invited her to use the Bannock facilities for training whenever she wanted. It had taken Daniel's death for everything to change.

She was an outstanding rider who'd been trained by her father. No barrel racer Connor had seen on the circuit this year had her speed and grace. He'd spotted her exceptional ability years earlier. Though she'd had a poor showing at her first professional rodeo, a lot of it had to do with the wrong horse.

Mac Henson, her father, had been an expert bull rider, but without financial support he hadn't been able to realize his dream of becoming a world champion. He had, however, turned his daughter into one by investing in a proper horse for her. Sunflower was a winner and could bring her a world championship.

"How would you like to drive to Las Vegas with me for the finals?"

Her lips broke into a sunny smile. "Ralph put you up to this."

No. His grandfather had nothing to do with it. Connor's invitation was his alone, but since she thought Ralph was behind it, what could it hurt? Maybe he'd have a better chance of getting her to say yes. He'd been planning to ask her for several months, but had to be careful not to give the impression he saw her as a charity case where money was concerned.

"In case you didn't know, he's sweet on you." That was only the truth.

Liz Henson was a brilliant horsewoman and had worked hard to get where she was. The least he could do to show support for a neighbor was to drive Sunflower there for the big event. Her dun-colored quarter horse had great speed. He liked her unusual yellowish-gray coat, which was set off by a black mane and tail. An original, like Liz herself.

Mac and Millie Henson hadn't made much money as foreman and housekeeper for that scrooge, Daniel Corkin, before he'd died. Now that they worked for Zane, there still wasn't a lot of money. Liz did have a job as a vet, but the practice wasn't lucrative. Even with the money she'd won so far this year, he knew she could use some physical help to get her to Las Vegas. He happened to know her equipment was ancient and liable to break down at any time along the way.

Connor realized his life had been blessed with many gifts. It would ease some of his guilt to use his means to do something for Liz, who had incredible talent. He was proud of her for making it to the national pro finals in Las Vegas. That was where they were both headed, since their wins at the Dodge Ram finals for the U.S. circuit region winners in Oklahoma City.

His grandfather was betting on her to win. So was Connor. With Daniel Corkin out of the way, Connor had decided he wanted to make things easier for her in the only way he knew how.

"That's very nice of both of you, but I've already made my arrangements. I'll be driving my truck and trailer."

Her answer sounded definitive. Connor figured she'd fight him at first, because she had spirit and was independent, like her folks, who were the salt of the earth. Connor had always liked the Hensons, too. But where Liz was concerned, it came to him that he'd have to fight fire with fire to get her to drive with him.

They'd been neighbors from birth, yet in all the intervening years he'd never spent time alone with her.

In fact, he'd never seen her when she wasn't wearing a cowboy hat and had a braid hanging down her back.

"If you don't accept my offer, it'll hurt my feelings."

She chuckled. "Since when?"

"You think I don't have any?"

Her brows formed a delicate frown. "I didn't say that."

"Good. It would mean a lot if you'll drive with me. Over the past few years I've seen you at a lot of the events and thought it ridiculous we didn't travel to them together. But because of Daniel's ban against all Bannocks, including you, I never tried to arrange anything."

"I'll admit he was a scary man, but that's over now."

"Since you said it, why don't you bury the proverbial hatchet and accept my offer. It'll be nice to have the company. We'll talk shop on the way down and celebrate our wins on the way back."

He was pleasantly surprised when her eyes lit up. "I like the way you think."

So far, so good. "I've made reservations at the RV park near the Mack Center. It has equestrian accommodations, and indoor and outdoor swimming pools. For the twelve days we're there, you and I will live out of my trailer while we're competing, whatever you want." It was the least he could do for his neighbor, and hopefully, friend.

LIVE WITH HIM? "I'm scheduled to stay at the Golden Nugget with the other barrel racers."

"I know, but you might like to be away from the others after your nightly events. I learned early I prefer being alone so nothing else gets into my head."

That was exactly the way she felt. The other competitors would be a distraction because they always wanted to go over the evening's events with a fine-tooth comb. Not staying with them might seem antisocial, but Connor had read her mind and had just given her priceless advice she'd be a fool not to take. "I hardly know what to say."

"Just say yes. But it's up to you. In case you didn't know, this is going to be my last event. After Las Vegas I'm through with competition."

"Sadie told me as much." Liz's best friend was married to Connor's brother and often confided in her.

"My new sister-in-law informed me this is going to be your last event, too."

Looks as if the confiding went two ways. "Yup. I've got to get serious about my career, but I have to admit I'm surprised about your decision." She smiled. "There are more good years left in the king of the bulldoggers."

"Those good years need to be spent doing more worthwhile things."

"That's an odd thing for you to say."

"The fact is, I've lived a selfish life so far, Liz."

She studied him for a moment, not understanding a comment like that. "What about Wade? You won't have room for three of us."

"Wade will be driving his horses down in his own trailer with his girlfriend, Kim. My traveling partners Shane and Travis will bring your second horse, Polly, and my other horse, Phantom, in my older rig with them. When they reach Las Vegas they'll stall them at the Mack Center tent for the rodeo. The guys will be over to pick up Polly whenever you give the word. We all like our own space."

He patted his horse's neck. "Since we need to be in Las Vegas by the third to attend the welcome celebrations before the first event on the fifth, I'm leaving early the day after tomorrow. Please say yes, otherwise I'm going to think Daniel did permanent damage to the relationship between our families."

He turned his horse to leave. When he reached the entrance, he looked over his shoulder at her. "I'll be listening for your call tomorrow. Just phone the ranch and I'll get back to you. Don't disappointment me. I'd rather not be alone with my own thoughts during the drive down and back, let alone throughout the competition." Without waiting for an answer, he left the arena.

Liz thought about his invitation all the rest of the day.

"Yoo-hoo!" she called to her mother when she got home from work.

"Is that you, honey?" Millie Henson always said that when Liz arrived.

"Who else?" she teased, and walked through the house to the kitchen.

"You're late. Your dad and I had Zane over for dinner an hour ago."

"I'm sorry."

"I was afraid something might have happened to your truck in this snow."

Liz stood at the sink to wash her hands. "I had to help with a birth at the Critchlow ranch. Mother and foal are doing well."

"That's good."

She turned to kiss her mom's cheek. "Something smells wonderful."

"Sit down and I'll serve you some roast chicken. I

tried that new recipe with the lemon and garlic from the food channel. The men said it's a winner."

"That's no surprise. You've never fixed a bad meal in your entire life."

Her mother drank coffee at the table with Liz while she dug into her meal. "This really is delicious, Mom."

"Thank you. Now, I want to talk to you about something serious. I'm worried about you driving all the way to Las Vegas in that old truck."

"It has enough life in it to get me to Nevada and back before it dies. But what if I told you I could drive there in total comfort?"

When Connor had told Liz he'd rather not be alone with his own thoughts, the statement had sounded lonely, troubled even. Before that he'd snapped, *You think I don't have feelings?*

Those two unexpected revelations in their conversation had made her decide to take him up on his offer, but telling her mom would only escalate her motherly concern. Still, they always talked things over. No matter what, there was honesty between them. Might as well get this over with right now.

Her mother put down her coffee mug. "Is Kyle taking you?"

"No."

"No?" She sounded disappointed. Her mom kept hoping Liz would meet the right man and settle down. "Then Sadie must have prevailed on Jarod to drive you."

Sadie's world had been transformed since she'd married Jarod Bannock six months ago. "They offered to take me, but I said no."

"That leaves Dr. Rafferty. Did he offer you the loan of his truck?"

"Yes."

"But you turned him down, too."

"I don't like being beholden to anyone."

"So you decided to rent a new truck. That's awfully expensive. I happen to know you've been saving your winnings to pay back your vet school loan."

"No, Mom." Liz put a hand on her mother's arm. "Early this morning Connor came by the arena and asked me to drive with him."

Like clockwork a shadow crossed over her mother's face. "Connor...as in Connor Bannock."

"Mom..."

Liz knew that came as a huge shock to her mother, who got up from the table. "You mean in his fancy hotel on wheels?"

"Unless he has to fly, it's the way he's been getting around for the past four years. It's not nearly as luxurious as some you see at the events. His handlers will bring Polly and his second horse down in his older rig. He's not a show-off, Mom, that much I do know about him."

He was all cowboy, tough and daring to the point that she often chewed her nails watching him shoot out of the barrier on his horse. He was so fast, his event was over before you could blink. Any pictures the journalists got of Connor had to be taken while they ran after him, because he never hung around after the required autographing sessions and photo shoots for his Wrangler sponsor. She and Sadie had often commented that both Bannock brothers were the least vain cowboys they knew.

"After all these years, why would he suddenly ask you now?"

Liz wanted an answer to that same burning question, but she said, "Ralph put him up to it. You *know* he did."

"I'm sure you're right about that, honey."

If Liz went with him, then she'd find out why he'd decided to honor his grandfather's wishes, but she'd known this would be her mother's reaction. Without hesitation she spent the next few minutes telling her the gist of their conversation at the arena. When she'd finished, Millie started to clear the dishes.

"Mom?" she prodded her.

"You're a grown woman, honey, and don't need my permission about anything."

Picking up her water glass, Liz took it over to put in the dishwasher. "I wasn't asking for permission," she said quietly.

Her mom turned to her with a sober expression. "You want my approval, otherwise you would have let me find out after the fact. But I don't want that responsibility. For years I watched you and Sadie grow up, both of you dying for love of the Bannock brothers. In Sadie's case, her love was reciprocated, whereas—"

"Connor hardly knew I existed and married someone else," Liz finished the sentence for her. Although they'd been neighbors, she'd never spent time alone with him, not even at the competitions. "Even having gone through a divorce, I doubt he's ever stopped loving her. Wasn't that what you were going to say?"

"Only that your infatuation with him has never ended," her mother murmured.

"You're right. I've been thinking about that all day. Infatuation isn't love. It's a crush I never outgrew. After all these years of being haunted by him, I have an opportunity for the first time to get a real dose of him, one-on-one. I'm convinced that driving to Las Vegas with him will be a revelation and provide the cure I've been needing."

"And if it isn't?"

Liz took a deep breath. "If it isn't, then I'll have to take a serious look at my life and make changes."

Her mother turned to look out the window. "That's what has me worried. Bannocks never pull up roots. That means you'll be the one who leaves us and move somewhere else."

"You're so sure of that? I'm thinking this will be my one and only chance to see who he really is and get over what has prevented me from moving on with another man."

A sigh escaped Millie's lips. "I only know one thing. I'm afraid to tell your father. He hasn't wanted anything to distract you before the competition. When he hears about this…"

Liz hugged her mom for a long time. "I'll talk to him and make him understand."

Chapter Two

Connor's black-and-silver horse trailer, hitched to his four-door black truck, contained everything you needed for comfortable living on the road. Two horse stalls with an extrawide floor and nonslip rubber matting, a niche with a bed and a sofa/pullout bed, a living/dining room, satellite TV, kitchen and bathroom, all in a nutmeg-colored wood with a ranch motif.

While Connor stashed her bags on board and showed her parents around, Liz took Sunflower's temperature one more time, and checked her eyes and nose before putting her in bell boots for protection during the journey. Now that the horse was ready to travel, she led Sunflower from the barn and loaded her into the trailer stall next to Firebrand.

Liz threw light rugs over each of them. Who knew whether the big sorrel gelding loaded in the roadside stall would like Sunflower's company or not? They were as unused to each other as Liz was to Connor. Despite the long journey ahead, Liz wasn't nervous and couldn't figure out why.

When she'd told her father she was going to drive with Connor, he'd been surprisingly supportive. "I'm glad you'll be with someone who's been hauling himself and his horse around for a long time. More snow is forecast over the whole intermountain region for the next few days. He's got the kind of equipment you need to keep you and Sunflower safe and comfortable."

Between the lines she read all the things he didn't say or warn her about. He didn't have to. She saw it in his eyes. Liz had the greatest parents on earth.

After she'd loaded her lightweight, high-horned saddle, she put the collapsible pop-up barrels she used for practice in the tack room of the trailer. She'd brought protein feed for her horse, wanting to keep a balance between forage and grain. Once she'd gathered her medical bag and stored it with everything, it was time to go.

She hugged her mom and then turned to her father. "I'm going to give it everything I've got to win, Dad. Thanks to you and Mom, and all your expert help, I think I have a chance."

"I know you do, Lizzie girl. Since Connor wants to win, too, I think you two are the best kind of company for each other. You already know what it's like to be in each other's skin, so to speak. You'll be able to offer each other the right sort of tips and comfort. Anyone not competing wouldn't know what you're facing, particularly when this competition will be the last for both of you."

Her dad understood everything.

"I can't believe this day is finally here."

He gave her that endearing lopsided grin. "Either you're growing up way too fast, or I'm getting too old."

"You're not getting old." She hugged him hard. *Please don't ever get old.*

"Your mom and I will fly down on the fourteenth

for the big night. Call us when you have a moment here and there."

"I'll call you when we get to Salt Lake tonight."

Connor had been standing close by and shook his head. "If the weather forecast is correct, we'll be lucky if we make it to the Utah border."

Her mom grabbed her one more time. "We'll be waiting to hear from you."

"I promise to stay in close touch."

"I love you, honey."

Tears stung Liz's eyelids. When she looked in her mother's eyes, she saw a whole world of love, fear, concern and pride. "Not as much as I love you," she whispered before climbing into the truck cab.

"I made some chili and rolls for you to enjoy on the way down. I put everything in the fridge."

"Thanks, Millie. We'll love it!" Connor called to her before she shut the door. His friends had already come to the barn to pick up Polly. Liz had given her a complete checkup first, and a treat, promising to see her soon. There was nothing left to be done.

Connor, wearing a green plaid shirt, jeans and well-worn boots, was already behind the wheel, ready to go. Minus the Stetson he'd tossed in the backseat, his hair had a disheveled look she'd seen often enough when he was wrestling a steer to the ground. That look suited him.

She wouldn't describe Connor as handsome in the traditional sense. *Authentic male* was what came to mind when she looked at the arrangement of lines and angles making up his hard-boned features.

Striking when the sun blazed down on his tanned skin.

Beautiful in motion when he mounted his horse bareback for a run.

Unforgettable when he flashed a quick smile or broke out in laughter, usually from some remark his friend Wade murmured at the gate so no one else could hear.

The kaleidoscope of pictures stored in her mind was there for good. Hopefully on this trip she'd see what was on the inside, the intangible traits that truly mattered and shaped the inner man. Was his inner self equally worthy of such admiration? If the cover of the book was better than the story, now was the time to find out.

Deep in thought, she didn't realize they'd pulled to a stop in front of the Bannock ranch house until Connor said, "Grandpa asked me if we'd come in so he could say goodbye and wish you luck."

"How sweet of him. I'd love to."

She jumped out into the snow and headed for the front porch. The temperature had to be close to thirty-two degrees. She zipped her parka all the way. It looked as though they'd be driving under an overcast sky most of the way today.

Connor opened the door and they headed for the den where they found his grandfather at his desk. The blaze from the fireplace gave out delicious warmth. The older man looked up with a smile and got to his feet. "Well, Liz."

"Hi again, Ralph." She hurried across the room to give him a hug. Liz had been here many times over the years.

"Connor told me you agreed to drive with him. Is he taking good care of you?"

"Of course. I'm a very lucky girl."

"It pleases me that my two favorite champions will be together. I have a little gift for the two of you." He pulled a small leather pouch out of his shirt pocket. "Avery picked it up for me on her way home from work yesterday."

Avery was Connor's sister. Liz couldn't imagine what the pouch could hold.

Connor's gaze shot to hers. "Go ahead and open it."

From inside the pouch she pulled out what looked like a silver charm bracelet. "You hang it on the rearview mirror of the truck to bring you luck. I chose the charms myself for this red-letter moment in your lives. See that horseshoe? Both of you have beaten me at the game any number of times. The next charm is a boot for riding. There's a cowboy hat. The others are a horse in motion, a bulldogger on his horse, a cowgirl barrel racing, and a heart with wings for love of country."

Liz was so touched that, once again, her throat swelled. "This gift is priceless, Ralph."

She noticed that Connor's eyes took on a haunted look when he glanced at his grandfather. *Why?*

"We'll treasure it."

"If Addie and your parents were here, son, they'd tell you and Liz to take it with our prayers and blessings. We've always been proud of both of you and know you'll do your best at the competition. We'll all be watching the Great American Country broadcast on cable. Whatever happens, come back safe. That's all I ask."

Full of emotion, Liz clutched the bracelet in her hand before reaching for him once more. "All we ask is that *you* stay well. I promised my folks we'd stay in close touch. We'll make the same promise to you. Without your help, I would never have made it this far. Whenever I got discouraged, you would never let me stay down."

"Ditto," Connor said in a husky tone of voice, and gave his grandfather a bear hug.

The older man whispered, "Good luck," to him, and a tear rolled down his cheek.

She waved to Ralph from the doorway. "See you soon." Without waiting for Connor, she hurried out of the house to the truck. He needed a minute with his grandfather, and she needed to treasure this special moment in private. Both she and Sadie had always loved Ralph and Addie. Like her own parents, she thought they were just about perfect.

Carefully she undid the chain clasp so she could hang the bracelet. To make certain it was visible, she draped it over the mirror. The little charms tinkled as they dangled.

A minute later Connor strode toward the truck and climbed in behind the wheel. He fingered one of the charms, and then flicked his gaze to hers. "Grandpa thinks the world of you to have given you this."

"Didn't you notice it's for both of us? Whenever he talks about you, his eyes light up."

An odd silence followed her remark. She didn't understand and wondered what he was thinking as he started the engine.

"Before we leave, is there anything you've forgotten?"

"If I have, it's not important."

"Bless you." Spoken like a man. She chuckled before he said, "Let's go."

They drove away from the ranch to the highway, cleared of snow since the storm the other night. "I'd like to reach North Salt Lake by evening. I made a reservation at the RV park on the outskirts with easy access."

"Sounds good to me. In case of more snow, I'd planned to drive as far as I could through Wyoming before finding a motel. I'm really grateful you asked me to come with you."

"Did you have someone to drive with you if I hadn't asked you?"

A vision of Kyle passed through her mind. She looked out the passenger window. "Yes. I had several offers from friends and family, but this is one trip I wanted to take alone. Knowing it's my last one, I didn't feel like sharing the experience with anyone else."

He sat back in the seat. "So how come you came with me?"

"Honestly?" she answered with another question.

"Shoot."

"Because you're not anyone else. When I told Dad I was driving with you, he said we were the best kind of company for each other since we already know what it's like to be in each other's skin."

"He was right."

"You've been to nationals and have won back-to-back world championships five times. Now you're trying for your sixth! This is my first time and you know exactly how vulnerable I'm feeling on the inside. I'm full of doubts and ambitions no else could understand, no one but someone like you, who's already experienced all those emotions and triumphed."

"That's the problem," he muttered. "No matter how many triumphs, you're only as good as your last one."

"I know. I find that out every time I compete at another rodeo."

"If you know that already, then you know a hell of a lot more than ninety-nine percent of your competition who believe their own hype."

His unexpected burst of emotion showed he felt as vulnerable as she did. Maybe more, because this would be his last competition. The need to prove himself one more time had to be testing his mettle in ways she couldn't fathom. No one would ever suspect that of Connor Bannock, the picture of confidence personified.

"In all honesty, I'm afraid, Connor," she admitted under her breath.

"Of failure?"

"A lot more than that. No matter what happens, I don't know what the future's going to be like without having a goal. I've been pursuing this dream for so long, it's taken up the hours of my world, consciously and subconsciously for years. Of course, I have my career, but that's different. I can't imagine what it will be like to wake up on December 15, knowing it's truly over…and the rest of my life is still ahead of me," she whispered.

"Lady, you just said a mouthful."

Liz turned her head toward him in surprise. "You *too?*"

"In spades."

SO FAR, NO snow had fallen, but it was coming. Connor felt the icy wind from a bleak sky while he and Liz

walked their horses at their first roadside park stop.
Two hours at a time was as much as their animals could
handle riding in the trailer. Their muscles got tired of
trying to maintain their footing and needed the rest.

With them tied up outside, he and Liz ate sandwiches and drank hot coffee in the trailer. Her earlier admission about thinking she'd be at a loss once
the competition was over was so in tune with his own
feelings, they seemed to have achieved a level of understanding that didn't require a lot of conversation.
He didn't feel the need to fill the gaps of silence. Neither did she.

By late afternoon, they'd made their fourth stop to
exercise the horses. Inside the trailer they both made
calls. He checked with Ben, the ranch foreman. Connor had hired a new hand to keep all the equipment on
the ranch in top shape. That had been Ned's job. Ben
sounded hopeful this new guy would work out. As they
talked, Connor could hear Liz talking to Dr. Rafferty
about a sick horse.

Once their phone business was done, they cleaned
up the stall floor before watering the horses and replen-
ishing their hay nets. Soon they'd brought the horses
back inside and were on their way again.

Since his quickie divorce from Reva Stevens two
years ago in Reno, he'd dated women, but he'd never
taken any of them on the road with him. This was a
first since the disastrous marriage in Las Vegas that
had only lasted a year. His grandfather had never said
anything, but Connor knew the older man hadn't been
happy about his impulsive marriage to the L.A. TV
anchor.

They'd made their base at her condo in L.A. When

he wasn't spending time with her, he traveled the rodeo circuit and worked on the ranch. She stayed on the ranch with him for a week after their honeymoon, but ranch life didn't hold her long. Both of them were too driven by ambition to put the other person first. The long separations took their toll, and divorce had seemed the only solution.

Though they hadn't been able to make it work, Reva called him from time to time. He kept their conversations short. He missed her in his bed. That had never changed, but it was everything else.

Liz's comment about being afraid of the future had resonated with him big-time.

Out of the corner of his eye he noticed her reading something on her iPad. "Anything interesting?"

"Yes. I've been checking stats. Dustine Hoffman just won the barrel-racing event at the Tom Thumb Texas Stampede in 13.71 seconds. She's everyone's competition."

He whistled. "That arena gives you faster time than the one in Las Vegas with its special soil."

She rolled her eyes at him. Between the dark lashes, they were as green as lime zest. He'd never seen eyes that exact color. "Thanks for trying to make me feel better. The truth is, she's a great athlete."

"So are you." Connor discovered that Liz had a great mouth, too. Soft and full, not too wide, but he couldn't afford to take his eyes off the road. "Didn't you do a 13.70 at Bakersfield?"

"I doubt I'll see a number that low again, but I can dream."

He knew all about that. "Did you read anything else interesting?"

A sly smile broke the corner of her mouth. "There must be a hundred blogs devoted to Connor Bannock. Your fans stretch around the country and back. Jocko Mendez from the Southeastern circuit in Arkansas is your closest competition, but word is out that Las Vegas is betting on you. Have you ever read any of them?"

She tried to get him off the subject of her.

"I don't have time." He let out a sigh. "Do yourself a favor and forget about Dustine Hoffman's stats. Concentrate on your routine with Sunflower. I watched you working with her the other morning. I'm impressed how well she body rates and changes leads between the first and second barrel."

"But I hear a but. What aren't you telling me?"

Liz was such a quick study, he needed to stay on his toes. "Am I that transparent?"

"Yes!"

He laughed. It was refreshing to be with someone who was too guileless to be anything but honest… unlike Reva, who'd harbored hurts and suspicions, then exploded at an unexpected moment.

"I notice you were working with wax reins, but they can be sticky. You have to really watch your hands with those. When they stick, you're pulling your horse around the barrel when you should be guiding her."

"Was that what I was doing the other morning?"

"No. I happened to notice it at your competition in Great Falls."

"You did?"

"Liz—we're not always at the same rodeos, but when we are, I make it a priority to watch my neighbor's performance."

She stirred in the seat. "I had no idea."

"When we get to Las Vegas, try using a knot rein at practice. They still slide when needed, but you might like the feel of them better. It's just a thought."

"But valuable input, coming from you. I'll try it."

One eyebrow lifted. "You're not offended?"

"By advice from *you?* What else did you see I can improve on?"

Connor decided she was like her dad, who didn't have a resentful, paranoid bone in his body. "Not a thing."

"Liar," she said with a smile, but it soon faded when stronger than usual gusts of wind buffeted the trailer. "Whoa—"

"Another storm front is moving in, but we're making good time so far. I'm glad we've reached Kemmerer. There's an RV park a mile away where I made a reservation, just in case. We may have to spend the night in Wyoming after all. I don't want to take chances with priceless cargo."

"You're right, of course. Our horses are precious."

"I was referring to you," he murmured.

Though she didn't dare take him seriously, her heart jumped anyway. "You sounded like your grandfather just then. Between your father and Ralph, you've had remarkable role models in them and it shows."

She saw his hands grip the steering wheel a little tighter. "You don't know my history. I'm afraid Grandpa has about given up on me."

There he went again. Something was going on where his grandfather was concerned, and she was curious. "Why would you say that? While he was hugging you, he had tears in his eyes, he's so proud."

"Those were tears of disappointment. I should have

quit the circuit several years ago in order to help him and Jarod."

Liz decided to take a risk. "Don't tell me your cousin Ned got to you, too, before he was put in that mental health facility—"

She heard his breath catch and knew she'd hit a nerve. "Sadie told me he about destroyed Jarod's confidence before they got back together. It sounds like he did a pretty good job on you, too. What did he tell you? That you didn't have what it took to run the Bannock ranch? Or did he make digs that you were running away from your responsibilities by letting the rodeo take over your life since your father's death?"

Connor stiffened. "I don't want to talk about it."

"You need to talk about it! Don't forget your grandfather was a rodeo champion in his day. He's in heaven watching you rack up the gold buckles."

Snow started to pelt the windshield, but she hardly noticed. "No doubt Ned accused you of leaving the work to your brother. Ned Bannock caused more trouble than Sadie's father ever did. Don't you know how jealous he was of you?"

Liz was all wound up and couldn't stop. "Ned never had your horsemanship and couldn't keep up with you. You were given a special gift. After you won your first buckle, why do you think he quit competing in rodeos so quickly? All he could do was undermine you, so you would feel guilty. He probably had a coronary when you married Reva Stevens, who looks like a movie star."

The windshield wipers were going full force while she kept on talking. "I'll bet he loved baiting you when you were divorced. Ned always did like to kick a man when he was already down. Well, I'd say he did a pretty fantastic job on you to make you feel like your grandfather is disappointed in you. But you would be wrong!

"Ralph adores you! I ought to know. I've been friends with him for years. If he's disappointed, then it's because he's afraid you've believed Ned. Shame on you, Connor!" Her rebuke rang in the cab.

By now, he'd turned into the RV campground and drove to the first place where they could stop. They were in a whiteout. But for the din of her voice, there was an eerie quiet. When she dared to look at him, his shoulders were shaking in silent laughter.

He turned in the seat, resting his head against the window where the snow was piling up and stared at her. "And here I thought you were a quiet little thing. But I should have known better after watching you on a horse. There's a spitfire inside of you. Feel better now that you've gotten it off your chest?"

Heat washed over her body in waves. "I'm sorry. I don't know what got into me."

His eyes played over her. "I don't think you left a thing unsaid. In fact, you mentioned a few things I hadn't even thought of that went straight to the gut." She wanted to crawl in a hole. "Who would have thought Liz Henson from the Corkin ranch, who's always in her own world, had so much insight?"

Always in her own world?

"I'm afraid Sadie and I spent a lot of time on the backs of our horses discussing Ned, who never left her alone. Worse, he never wasted a chance to berate his cousins in front of us and any audience who happened to be around. It wasn't just Jarod he hated. He had plenty to say about you.

"When you trained Firebrand, a feral no one else could handle, he was furious at your success. Worse, every girl on the Montana circuit would have given her eyeteeth to go out with you and *he* knew it."

"Not every girl," he said in a quiet voice.

"You mean Sadie, but we both know why."

"I meant *you,* Liz."

"Me—?"

Connor cocked his head. "Don't you remember the time I asked you if you wanted to celebrate with me after you won at the Missoula Stampede?"

Liz blinked. "I figured you asked me for Wade's sake in order to set us up."

"He has a girlfriend now."

"I'm glad. He's kind of shy. Though I've always liked him, I was never interested in him that way."

"Ouch. Now you've wounded him *and* me."

"What do you mean *you?* You were married."

"Nope. Divorced. If you'd agreed, I would have told you I was single again, but you didn't give me the time of day. Before you shut me down cold, I figured we were far enough away from home that old man Corkin wouldn't find out the off-limits neighbors were getting friendly."

Her heart thudded. "Even if I had known the change in your marital status, I wouldn't have said yes. Being in love with the woman you married doesn't go away because of a piece of paper. Jarod and Sadie were still head over heels in love after eight years, even after she wrote him that awful goodbye letter he actually believed, and all because of Ned!"

"That's a fact." Connor reached to shut off the engine. "I think your explanation for rejecting me has helped a little."

"Give it up, Connor," she teased with a chuckle.

"I'll keep everything you told me in mind and cogitate on it."

"You do that."

"What do you say we go back to the trailer and enjoy some of your mom's chili while we see how long this storm is going to last."

WHILE SHE WARMED up their food, Connor put on his hat and jacket before walking back to check on the horses. The wet snow was coming down fast. The horses were better off inside their stalls where it was warm. He didn't want them catching a cold and made sure they had what they needed before he headed for the trailer.

He shook off the snow before entering. When he saw her seated at the kitchen table, a sense of guilt swept over him. Not for the things she'd deduced about his troubled psyche, which were right on, but because he hadn't given her life the same amount of thoughtful attention she'd given his. Most of the time he'd been too immersed in his own problems to think of others. He was the opposite of his grandparents.

They knew all about Sadie's and Liz's dreams, but they'd never divulged the essence of their conversations with Connor. His grandparents were saints who worried about everyone and did the little things that endeared them to friends and family. Take that charm bracelet. Connor had seen the loving expression on her face for Ralph. It came from the heart.

After hanging up his hat and jacket, he moved to the table. She immediately got to her feet to wait on him and pour him a mug of hot coffee. The one time he'd traveled with Reva in his trailer, to an event within California, she'd sat there waiting for him to take care of her. Even then, she'd insisted on staying nights at a hotel with room service.

She'd told him she really didn't like the trailer. It was too claustrophobic for her. Reva liked to eat out. So did he, once in a while. He excused her because he knew it simply wasn't her lifestyle. But the time came when just about everything he did or suggested didn't appeal to her.

They didn't grow together in their marriage. Through no true fault on either part, their physical attraction couldn't take care of everything else that was wrong. Starting a family had been out of the question. But enough dredging up the past he preferred to forget.

After eight hours of driving it was still so pleasant being with Liz, he kept wondering when the spell would wear off and she'd turn into someone else.

"Eat while the chili's hot. Mom made some rolls, too." Liz passed the plate to him. He took three.

"Thank you. I've been salivating for this all day."

"Me, too. How are our children by the way? Do you think they're getting along all right in such close quarters?"

Connor chuckled at the charming way she'd put it. "They were both quiet."

"They've never been stalled together. Sunflower is probably missing Polly and vice versa."

"This is a new experience for Firebrand, too. I don't know if they're being shy or bored."

"Wouldn't it be interesting if horses had romantic feelings...."

When he looked into her eyes, they were smiling. "Since when did White Lodge's newest vet delve into horse psychiatry?"

"Since the time Sadie told me about Chief, Jarod's stallion. He had a harem when he ran wild in the mountains. That got me thinking."

A burst of full-bodied laughter broke from him. "Maybe by the time the rodeo's over, we'll find out Firebrand and Sunflower have become inseparable."

She grinned. "You have to admit it would be amazing. I'd write it up in the *Journal of American Veterinary Medicine.* At our last stop, I noticed Firebrand sniffing around Sunflower's dung. Did you know feral horses like yours are fascinated by the dung piles of other horses?"

He tried not to laugh, but couldn't help it. "I have to admit I didn't."

"It's true. Dung and urine from other herds act as newspapers from one herd to another. Just what is communicated through urine and dung is unknown, but it may communicate how healthy the herd is, what mares are in season and even what types of food is available in the area."

"Let's be thankful her heat cycle ended after September. Otherwise, we'd know it by now."

Liz laughed gently. "Never fear. When I compete at the wrong times, I give her a medication so there's no problem. So…if these two get interested in each other, it won't be because of hormones."

Connor eyed her thoughtfully. "Just pure chemistry."

"Wouldn't *that* be something." She sounded bemused.

"Indeed it would." But his mind wasn't on the

horses. The woman seated across from him had drawn his attention. She wore her usual braid, but it lay forward over her shoulder, brushing against her flushed cheek while she drank her coffee. He could pick out the sun streaks in her light chestnut hair.

The collar of her tan Western blouse lay open at the throat. It came to him she had no idea how truly lovely she was. There was nothing artificial about her. If she wore makeup right now, he couldn't tell. She didn't need it.

"More chili?"

He handed her his bowl. "Please."

"You don't know how happy it will make Mom to hear you liked it." She got up from the table, giving him a profile view. Liz had to be five foot seven, with a supple body filling out her blouse and jeans in all the right places. With those long legs, she made quite a sight astride her horse during a competition.

His thoughts flicked to Reva, who was five foot four and more voluptuous. But she didn't move with the same grace as Liz, who was in fabulous shape from working and riding horses all her life.

Connor wouldn't be a man if he hadn't noticed, but it had always been at a distance. His grandfather had begged him to stay away from the Corkin ranch so there'd be no trouble. He had obeyed him, effectively putting Liz out of reach over the years.

Since then, she'd become a doctor of veterinarian medicine. No doubt she'd have to work years to pay off her loan for medical school. Besides the gold buckle, she'd win the big money, so maybe she could buy a new truck. More than ever he wanted her to be able to take those prizes home. No one deserved them more than she did. The relic she'd been driving was on its last legs.

He was glad she'd come with him. The storm hadn't let up. It could snow another hour or two, but they and their horses were safe and cozy inside the trailer. His mood had been dark for the past few months despite his wins, but right now he felt a lifting of his spirits and liked the feeling.

Connor got to his feet and took his dishes over to the minikitchen. "What do you say we give the horses a little exercise now?"

"I can see you're dying to find out how they're getting along."

"Aren't you?"

She flashed him an intriguing smile before putting on her parka and gloves. Her black cowboy hat came last. After he put on his gear, they walked out into a white world. The snow wasn't coming down as hard, but it was steady. Like a child, she put her head back to catch some snowflakes on her tongue, reminding him of his youth. He hadn't had this much fun in a long time.

Connor opened the back of the trailer and they walked inside. Both of them spoke in low tones to their horses as they led them outside for some exercise. After they'd gone a distance, they stopped.

"It feels like we're in wonderland." She half laughed the words. "Look, Connor. Did you see what Sunflower just did when Firebrand smelled her breath?"

He couldn't say that he had because he'd been looking at the expression of delight on her face. "What did I miss?"

"Sunflower's head lifted in the air and she lowered

her ears. See how she's chewing on the air? That's a submissive gesture in front of Firebrand because she recognizes his higher rank. Her foal-like behavior is so sweet. I think they really do like each other!"

Connor patted his horse's neck. "Is that true, buddy? Are you falling for Sunflower?"

A nicker came out of his horse, followed by one from hers.

"I swear he understood you!"

"Maybe they've been giving each other tips."

Her amused gaze met his, sending an emotional response through him he hadn't expected. How was it that Liz had been his neighbor for twenty-six years, yet it had taken until now to start seeing inside this attractive woman who he already knew had the heart of a champion?

"You mean about racing?"

"And other things…"

Gentle laughter escaped her throat. "You think they're making plans for after we leave them alone for the night?"

"Something like that. Firebrand hasn't been around such a fetching little mare in a long time. Being gelded doesn't mean he's forgotten anything."

Her eyes sparkled through the falling snow. "Come to think of it, Firebrand's Spanish heritage is pretty exciting, with those horizontal zebra stripes on the backs of his forelegs. His coloring is unique, even among ferals. It gets a female thinking."

He moved closer to her. It brought the horses closer together. "And here I thought it was only the male who was a leg man."

"You'd be surprised what captures the attention of the female."

"What else, for example?" he drawled.

"Oh, the white star on Firebrand's forehead and his dorsal stripe. And he's a powerful size. Makes a female feel protected. Notice how she's been scratching him on the rump with her teeth? She likes being around him."

"He likes a good scratch."

Her arched brows lifted. "Well, he's getting one. Amazing she knew where he itched."

"Lucky him. Who would have thought being stuck out in the back of beyond during a blizzard he would find such bliss?"

"It proves pure chemistry can work anywhere, but I think we'd better take them in. I want to check their gums and temperatures."

"If they both have a fever, we'll know romance is definitely in the air."

As she walked ahead of him with Sunflower, her laughter rippled back to tease his senses. He followed her into the trailer. After they'd dried off the horses, she gave them a thorough checkup while he cleaned the floor and put out fresh water and hay.

They worked as a team. No unmet expectations. No trauma of any kind. No deadlines. All that lay ahead of them was the rest of the night together. Nothing could have suited him better.

"It's still coming down, Liz. We're going to have to stay here until morning. By then the highway will have been plowed and we'll have a straight shot to Salt Lake. Depending on the weather tomorrow, we might make it to Las Vegas by nightfall."

"I'm glad we're not taking chances. Our horses need

special handling at a time like this if we expect the very best from them in the arena."

"Amen."

She threw the light rugs over them. "They look good and are probably wishing we'd leave them alone. Okay, guys. Treat time." She reached in her parka for some Uncle Jimmy's Squeezy Buns. She gave a few to Connor to give his horse.

"Did you see that? Sunflower starts talking when she hears the wrapper being opened. I swear she'd drool if she could."

Another chuckle came out of Connor, who fed Firebrand. After they'd finished their chores, he followed Liz out of the back. Just before he closed things up, he heard more nickering between both horses. Liz's mouth curved into a mischievous smile. "I'd say all is well."

Yup. Everybody was happy. It surprised him how much he was looking forward to more time alone with her.

The ringing of his cell phone broke the magic of the moment, preventing him from responding. He pulled it from the pocket of his jeans to check the caller ID.

Reva? He might have known. She knew how to choose her times.

Damn.

"Go ahead and take it while I clean up the kitchen." She hurried around the end of the trailer. Liz couldn't have known who was calling, but good manners stopped her from asking questions or lingering. Not that he'd been trying, but so far he hadn't found anything wrong with her. Quite the opposite, in fact.

He could talk to his ex-wife now or call her back later. The choice was his. But in that moment, while he was deciding what he wanted to do, he realized more than ever how much his feelings had changed since they'd been divorced. The old Connor wouldn't have let it ring a fifth time.

Before long she'd left him a text message.

Connor? Know u r on the road. Want u to know I'll be in Las Vegas tomorrow.

No way. He had no desire to see her while he was there to compete. There was no time for her. He and Wade had their horses to exercise and take care of.

I took off work. Have reserved honeymoon suite at the Mirage. Hope to give our marriage another try.

Where was this coming from? Something new had to be going on in her life. Maybe she'd broken up with the television producer she'd been dating since their divorce. Some kind of change was in the works. He knew Reva. For them to reconnect, she'd have to leave Los Angeles, because ranching was his life. She hated ranch life. If he didn't know anything else, he knew that.

She'd had two years to think about it. So had he, but he wasn't sure if he wanted her back, even if she gave up her television career and agreed to live with him on the ranch. Two years had changed him, and would have changed her. It would mean starting over again.

He doubted she would ever get the show biz bug out of her system. Connor couldn't blame her for that, any more than he could stamp the rodeo bug out of his blood. She was pursuing her dreams. With the right marriage she could go on doing it.

Key at front desk. Let yourself in. Middle of night doesn't matter. Dying to see you, lover. Miss u more than ever.

Connor couldn't honestly say the same. What was going on with her?

The snow kept falling.

Shielding his phone, he replied with his own text message.

Reva? May not make Las Vegas by tomorrow. Can't stay at Mirage. Give u a call later.

The Mirage was home to the NFR steer wrestlers, but she knew he preferred staying in his own trailer. After he put the phone back in his pocket, he walked around to the entrance. Shaking more snow off everything, he stepped inside and hung his things up. No sign of Liz, which meant she was in the bathroom. She'd cleaned up the kitchen. Her appeal was growing on him in ways he hadn't anticipated.

He washed his hands and poured himself another cup of coffee. While she was busy, he phoned Wade. He and Kim had made it to Evanston. So far, so good. They talked about the weather for a minute before hanging up.

He made one more call, to his grandfather, who sounded relieved to hear Connor's voice. After assuring him that he and Liz were fine, Connor asked how Ralph's day had gone. That was when he learned Ned would be coming home tomorrow for a supervised overnight visit. His first since being at the mental health facility.

Connor put his coffee down. "Does Jarod know?"

"Yes. I told him that he and Sadie ought to go out to the reservation while he's here."

"Good plan. You don't want anything to go wrong that could set him off."

"According to the doctor, Ned is making a turn-around. We're all keeping our fingers crossed."

"I will, too."

"Bless you, son. What you need to do is keep concentrating on the competition. Tell me about the little princess." That was what Ralph had always called Liz.

"She's a great vet and terrific company." All of it true. But he'd already found out she was a lot more than that.

"That's what I needed to hear. I assured her father you were taking good care of her."

"We're taking good care of each other. Let him know Millie's chili and rolls were a sensation."

"I'll tell him." After a silence, "Son?" Connor heard him hesitate. "Reva called the house earlier. I told her you were already on your way to Las Vegas."

He gripped his phone tighter. "She texted me." Connor could hear the question his grandfather didn't ask. It was the question Connor couldn't answer.

Ralph never pried. That was what made him so lovable.

"I'll call you tomorrow night, Grandpa. Maybe by then you can tell me how the visit went with Ned. Sleep well and don't worry about a thing."

"Ha! Just wait till one of your grandchildren tells you the same thing."

That last comment stayed with him as he hung up the phone. Since the divorce, he couldn't see himself having children, let alone grandchildren. Much to his grandfather's disappointment, as well as Connor's own personal pain, that didn't appear to be in his future.

Right now he didn't want to think about it.

Chapter Three

"Connor? Is everything all right?"

His head jerked up.

Liz had just come out of the bathroom in her new nautical-design pajamas in navy with polka dots on the bottoms. She'd washed her hair and had braided it again.

"Perfect," he said automatically, but she didn't believe him. "Where do you want to sleep? Up in the niche or near the floor? Both are comfortable."

"I think the sofa pullout bed." It was closer to the bathroom and the kitchen if for any reason she had to get up in the night. In the back of her mind she imagined Connor had probably slept with Reva in the niche with its pull-down ladder.

"Good. I'll take my shower now. By the way, I had keys made for you to open the trailer and the truck. I put them there on the counter."

"That was very considerate. Thank you."

"Anything to oblige."

By his tone of voice, something was wrong and it worried her.

She turned on the TV to the weather channel and then made her bed. To her surprise, his low-profile satellite dish was still allowing transmission despite the snow. The forecast predicted more intermittent flurries through Wyoming and the northern half of Utah tomorrow, but the southern half would be warmer and might see a little sun. Las Vegas was enjoying sixty-three-degree weather during the day and lower forties at night with some wind.

Liz still couldn't understand why she didn't feel uncomfortable in this situation. Maybe it was because they both knew so much about each other's lives, there was no mystique. Connor didn't feel like an acquaintance or a confidante, brother, cousin, best friend or boyfriend.

He existed outside those categories, though he wasn't a figment of her imagination. She didn't know what he was, but so far the inside of the book matched the cover. That didn't bother her, either. Curious.

Once under the blanket, she made a call home and thanked her mom for the food. Liz assured her parents that she and Connor were snug as a bug in his trailer while they waited out the storm in Kemmerer. The horses were in great shape. Connor was an expert— behind the wheel or mounted on his horse.

"Good night, you two. Thank you for being the greatest parents on earth."

When she clicked off, she discovered Connor standing there in a pair of navy sweats. Their nightwear more or less matched. She could smell the soap he'd used in the shower. She'd left hers and he'd used it.

"Your parents are very trusting, you know that?"

"Besides the fact that you're one of *the* famous Bannock brothers, don't forget I was away at vet school for a long time and am not exactly a little girl anymore."

"No, you're not." His emphatic tone sent a shiver through her before he picked up the remote and flipped the channels to an old creature-of-the-lagoon movie. After tossing it to her, he turned out the light and climbed into the niche using the same masterful agility with which he threw a steer. She laughed when he got comfortable and looked down at her over the edge. "Monsters don't scare you?" His mood had improved.

"Not really, if that was your intention. I'm laughing because I meant *this*. I'm having fun. Being in the trailer is like we're in a little hut deep in the forest of some mysterious kingdom."

"With satellite TV, no less." His sudden smile turned him into the most attractive man she'd ever laid eyes on. "In truth, I'm having more fun than I've had in years, stranded with a vet who's writing a romance article about the mating rituals of horses. After it's in print and you've won the prize for the world champion barrel racer, what do you plan to do for an encore?"

She raised herself on one elbow. "Mind if I try something out on you?"

"What do you think? Go ahead."

"Well, the Crow council in Pryor has asked me if I'll be one of the vets for the reservation. Even if Jarod had everything to do with the offer, it's such a great honor I can hardly believe it. But I haven't given them my answer yet because I'm committed to Dr. Rafferty at the vet hospital. I'd have to stretch myself thin to do both."

He rested his chin on his hard-muscled arm. "And here I thought you were worrying about what you were going to do with the rest of your life once the rodeo was over. Winning money to buy a new truck is going to come in handy with you driving back and forth from White Lodge to the reservation."

"Don't I wish! In order to win it, I'll have to beat Dustine's time along with several other unknowns at the moment. That's a tall order."

"You're the best barrel racer on the circuit this year, Liz. In my official opinion, you're a shoo-in. To the winner goes all the pickings."

"Thanks for the morale boost, Connor." She patted her pillow. "As long as we're talking about the future, after you've won your sixth title, have you thought about getting involved with the Pryor Mountains National Wild Horse Refuge?"

He laughed. "*What* did you say? I don't think I heard you correctly."

"Oh, I think you did." She egged him on. "When you rescued and adopted Firebrand, you got yourself a real prize. The horse refuge needs people like you. Your voice would carry a lot of weight, politically."

A look of surprise crossed his face. "Are you a lobbyist, too?"

"I'm just a vet who's an interested bystander and would love to see someone like you, with real clout, protecting Montana's natural resources. It's the second feral horse refuge in the U.S. Gus Cochran, one of the leading equine geneticists, concluded that the Pryor herd may be the most significant wild-horse herd remaining in the States. These animals don't exist anywhere else, and they need advocates."

He held himself so still, she realized she had his attention.

"Do you remember Wild Horse Annie, a secretary at an insurance firm in Reno?"

"I know of the Wild Horse Annie Act."

"Well, she was obviously a wild horse advocate who lobbied for passage of a federal law to prevent hunting the herds from helicopters, and motorcycles that terrorized the horses and caused extreme cruelty."

"Amen to that."

"Because of her, the Hunting Wild Horses and Burros on Public Lands Act was passed in the late fifties, banning the hunting of feral horses on federal land using aircraft or motorized vehicles."

"You learn something new every day. Tell me more," he urged with a genuine smile.

His honest interest pleased her. "Seven years ago, the last three slaughterhouses in the U.S. were closed, all because certain interested parties discovered that some of the excess wild horses being sold had been sent straight to the slaughterhouses and killed."

He shook his head, signaling his disgust.

"When they intervened, the BLM had to suspend the sales program. After investigating, they resumed the sales, but only after implementing new requirements to deter buyers from killing the animals.

"There's a ton of work to be done for their preservation. Your grandfather has a huge ranching reputation in the state. For his prominent grandson, Connor Bannock, to get involved in the fight to preserve the very kind of horse that will bring you another victory in the arena… It would be doing a great thing for man, horse and country. Of course, you'd have to do that work along with your regular ranch work. It would be stretching you to the max, too."

The next instant Connor swung himself to the floor with masculine ease and hunkered down in front of her. His brown eyes searched hers for a full minute. "What's behind all this?" He was asking a serious question.

"Ever since you started working with Firebrand, I've wanted to talk to you about it. He's a very special horse, and you knew it right away. Not everyone has an eye for good horseflesh like you. Ralph said your father was the same. It seems you inherited that trait. I understand it was while he was looking over the best horses on the reservation that he met Jarod's mother."

"That's true."

"If you were to salvage a couple more stallions like Firebrand, you could start your own stud farm. The filly Jarod gave Sadie came from Chief, another feral. Think about it!"

His brows furrowed. "Where did that idea come from?"

"From you! Before your parents died, Sadie and I were over in your backyard throwing horseshoes with Ralph. We happened to overhear you tell Jarod you wanted to establish a stud farm to bring in more money. I thought it was a fabulous idea, but then your folks were killed. I could see you had your hands full with the regular ranch work and your grief."

"That was a terrible time," he whispered.

"I know, but I've thought about your idea ever since. Do you realize your stud farm would be unique if you advertised that you only used adopted feral stallions? There are horse lovers everywhere who'd be excited for a foal from a sire like Firebrand. You'd be preserving the bloodline of horses that have roamed these mountains for centuries. It gives me chills just to think about it."

"You're not the only one." He showed her his arms with raised bumps. She couldn't believe it. "I had no idea you heard me," he murmured, "let alone that you would still remember."

"We hadn't meant to eavesdrop, but both of us thought you should do it. You wouldn't have any competition."

He cocked his dark blond head. "Where have you been all my life, Liz Henson?"

"Right next door, working on my dream to be a barrel racer."

"You worship your dad, don't you?"

He could see right through her. She nodded. "He should have been able to realize his dream to be a pro bull rider, but it didn't happen."

"So you're doing this for him."

"Probably somewhere inside I am. He had to work so hard for everything all his life. Daniel Corkin was not an easy taskmaster."

"No."

"My parents couldn't have more children. I was it, and I was a girl. He needed a son. All I could do was be the best at something and decided to try barrel racing. Mom encouraged me because she knew what it meant to him. Sadie raced with me."

"Don't take me wrong, but your talent surpassed hers and everyone else's at those early rodeos. All you needed was the right horse."

"Thank you."

"There was never any jealousy between the two of you, was there?"

"Or between you and Jarod. If you must know, my mother suffered over not being able to have another baby. That's why she was so happy when Sadie turned to her for everything after her parents' divorce. With Sadie's mom in California, there was no one else to love her except our family. Sadie was a sweetheart. Still is."

Connor's eyes grew suspiciously bright. "I agree, but I have to say you've been blessed with exceptional parents, Liz. There's nothing I'd like more than to see their little girl take the prize in Las Vegas. I'm here for you in any capacity you need." His voice throbbed with emotion she could feel clear through to her insides. "Ask anything of me and I'll do it if it's within my ability."

"Connor—" she put a hand on his arm "—driving me to Las Vegas is the greatest thing you could have ever done for me. You've taken away the burden of getting my horse there by myself. Now I can concentrate."

"That's good. You need to feel relaxed." He checked his watch. "I'm keeping you up when you need sleep. Do you want the TV on?"

"If you want to watch a program, that's fine with me. If not, turn it off." She let go of his arm to hand him the remote.

He clicked off the TV and put the remote on the table before returning to his niche.

Liz lay there in the dark, wide-awake. The wind had died down. All was quiet. Her thoughts drifted to Connor. She'd never slept in the same room with a man before. When she'd accepted his invitation, she'd done it to find out what the real Connor was like.

Already she'd discovered he was thoughtful and kind in ways she wouldn't have expected. Hidden in the many layers was a sense of humor. Buried even deeper lived a sensitive, vulnerable man. All this she'd learned, and it was only the first day.

As for the damage his divorce had done to him, she didn't know, but she envied the woman who was loved by him....

"Liz?"

Her pulse raced. "Yes?"

"Who's the lucky guy in your life?"

She smiled. "Dad says they're all lucky."

"All?" After a pause, "Why aren't you with your favorite?"

"They're all my favorites for different reasons, but as I told you this morning, I wanted to be alone this trip. The fact that I'm with you doesn't count."

"Why?" He sounded a little tense.

"Because in my mind you're not animal, vegetable or mineral."

"Thanks a lot."

"I haven't finished. You're beyond all that."

"In other words, you view me as an extraterrestrial."

"No. You're an entity who has always floated around in the background of my life. I think that's why I don't find it strange being with you."

"You mean I'm like the specter that never went away."

A chuckle escaped her lips. "No. *You* have substance and form."

"I'm feeling better already."

"Go to sleep, Connor. You need it much more than I do."

"Hey—I'm not an old man yet."

"Age has nothing to do with it. You've done all the

driving. I'm beholden to you. The only way to pay you back is to feed you and let you rest."

"Did you bring any treats?"

"If I give you one, will you promise to go to sleep?"

"I can't promise to do that, but I'll stop talking."

"Hallelujah!"

He burst into laughter as she got out of bed and padded over to the kitchen. After retrieving a Snickers candy bar from the sack, she hurried back and lifted it to him. "Enjoy. You can work off the calories later."

Connor grabbed her hand and held on. "Want to split it with me?"

"I can't. I just brushed my teeth."

She tried to get away but he tugged harder. Liz had a hunch she was going to pay for teasing him.

"You can brush them again. I don't like having a midnight snack by myself. Come on up." Before she knew what had happened, he'd lifted her onto the edge of the bed so her feet dangled. His strength in throwing steers accounted for the ease with which he'd brought her up to his level.

"Here." He broke the bar in half and handed her a piece. "Partners in sin." Between the adrenaline rush he'd given her and the sugar, she'd be awake for the rest of the night. "Good, huh?"

Liz's mouth was full of chocolate. She made a sound of assent.

"As you can see, I not only have form and substance, I can eat, too."

"I'm convinced!" she finally managed to say.

"Then I'm making progress."

Yes. Way too much.

"Good night, Connor." She jumped down before he could stop her. One more second up there...

She didn't dare think about it. Her father had commented that it would be good for them to travel together because they knew what it was like to be in each other's skin.

But once under the covers, she had one more thing to add to this day of revelations. He'd almost charmed her right out of hers.

SMOKEY'S STEAK HOUSE in St. George, Utah, lay straight ahead. Connor looked over at Liz. "Hungry?"

"Starving."

"So am I. They serve a great steak. I've been here dozens of times."

After being on the road all day with stops to take care of the horses, they needed a hot, filling meal. Because of the snow, they'd gotten away from Kemmerer later than he'd wanted. The highway had looked like a snow-covered pasture instead of a road in spots, which had cost them a couple of hours in time. However once they got past Cedar City, Utah, the highway was clear.

They could make it to Las Vegas tonight, but it would be eleven at night before they pulled in. Connor preferred to spend the night at an RV park here and arrive tomorrow during daylight. Reva was probably at the Mirage now, expecting he would break down and come to the hotel, but that wasn't going to happen.

To his surprise, for the first time in years he felt as if he was on a real vacation and wanted it to go on and on. The ten days of competition coming up hadn't caused his stomach muscles to cramp. Maybe there was something wrong with him to feel this relaxed.

Liz had brought a couple of books on tape that they listened to during the drive. It was a nice change from music he got tired of listening to. He'd enjoyed both books very much and had finished off another Snickers bar during their lively discussions about the new theories behind Kennedy's assassination. There was always another version of what really happened.

When he'd parked their rig, Liz excused herself to use the restroom inside the restaurant, and he watched her walk toward it. Cowboy boots on the right pair of long shapely legs along with hips encased in jeans were a sight to behold all on their own. Her braid swung back and forth against the back of her fitted suede jacket. He noticed she'd drawn the eyes of several interested males in the parking area.

The temperature here was sixty-one degrees, so he didn't bother with a coat. His sweater would do. Putting on his hat, he walked back to check on the horses. Their ears pricked the moment they heard noise.

"Hi, guys. How's the romance coming?" More nickering out of both. He smiled. "After our dinner, we'll take care of you."

He closed the door and headed into the crowded restaurant. Liz had found them a booth by a window. Cozy, just like the trailer. Their eyes met. "I'll wash my hands and join you."

"Take your time. How are the children?"

"They told me to hurry."

She laughed. "I think they can't wait to be outside together."

"It wouldn't surprise me." His good mood stayed with him until he was returning to their booth and saw a couple of guys talking to Liz. One of them turned in his direction.

"Connor! We saw you pull up in your rig."

If it wasn't the Porter brothers from Rock Springs, tough competitors on the circuit in team roping. As siblings they had instincts that guaranteed them another championship. Both were friends of Wade's from their college days and had spent part of an evening with Connor and Reva in Las Vegas after they were married.

"Hey, guys." They shook hands. "I take it you've met this year's soon-to-be barrel-racing champion, Dr. Elizabeth Henson."

"We're working on it," Monty said with a grin.

Derrick asked, "You mean, besides chasing the cans, you're a doc? I've got a sore leg I'd like you to look at."

"She's a vet," Connor inserted before Liz could. Odd that he felt so territorial.

"That's good, too," Monty commented. "Our horses need a good going-over." His brows lifted. "Is Reva still out in the trailer?"

Time to get this over with. "We're divorced," he said.

"Whoops." Monty looked embarrassed. "I'm afraid we didn't hear about that," he murmured.

"How could you have known?"

They probably hadn't because they competed in the Mountain States circuit. But the fact that Wade hadn't gossiped about Connor's private life to other people raised the man even more notches in his estimation.

"We were going to ask if you wanted to join us, but under the circumstances we'll find ourselves another booth."

"Thanks, Monty." Connor didn't feel like sharing Liz. "Good to see you, too, Derrick."

"Going for your sixth title has already made you a legend. Good luck, Connor."

"The same to you. This could be your third."

"We're hoping."

He turned to Liz. "Ma'am. If Connor says you're a winner, then you can believe him." They tipped their hats to Liz, their eyes lingering on her before they walked off.

The moment he sat down across from her, the blond waitress came to take their order.

"They were nice," Liz said after the woman walked away.

"Wade met them in college."

"I saw them in action at the arena in Oklahoma. They're fast."

"In a lot of ways," he informed her. His comment produced another chuckle. "If you want, I'll find them. They wanted to join us, but I didn't know how you'd feel about that."

"I'm glad you didn't take them up on it."

He squinted at her. "I bet you get hit on all the time."

"I don't get the attention *you* get. So far, every waitress in here has passed by our table, even when it isn't their area. They all know who you are. Ours was salivating over you. No doubt she'll serve you a free dessert and invite you for drinks later."

Connor started to laugh. "The things you say, Liz Henson, and the times you pick to say them."

"If the truth fits… Please do what you want."

His jaw hardened. "I don't party or drink except for an occasional beer with Jarod or Wade. Ned's alcoholism cured me of that problem early in life."

Her eyes softened. "I didn't mean to upset you, Connor. I just wanted you to feel free to do whatever you want."

"You're too good to be true, you know that?"

"Is *that* what I am? I thought traveling with you in your trailer was a pretty daring move on my part."

"How could it be daring when you only think of me as an entity?" He hadn't forgotten how she'd shocked him when she'd jumped down from his bed last night before he could think.

"With substance, form and an appetite for candy bars," she added with a twitch of her lips, enticing him. "At this point I have to add deep-seated feelings to the list I'm making on you."

"A list?" Connor liked the sound of that.

His cell phone rang, intruding on his personal thoughts. Much as he wanted to ignore it, he didn't dare in case something was wrong with his grandfather. He reached in his pocket and pulled it out to check the caller ID. One look and he put it back.

By now, their dinner had arrived. He thanked the waitress without looking at her. He'd been happy until they'd come into the restaurant. Now everything felt out of kilter. They ate in silence. When he saw the waitress coming again, he asked Liz, "Do you want dessert?"

"Oh, no. That steak did it for me."

"Then let's get going."

He pulled out his credit card and handed it to their server without waiting for her to talk. She'd looked as though she was about to say something, then thought the better of it. "I'll be right back."

A glimmer of amusement lit Liz's eyes. "You disappointed her."

"She'll get over it."

"Connor—you can't blame a gal for trying."

"How come you didn't have that compassion for me when you turned me down flat in Missoula?"

A shadow broke out on her face. "That was different. I thought you were a married man, but you already know that."

"It still hurt. We were neighbors." He wrote the tip on the receipt the waitress had brought back with his credit card. When she left the table he pocketed it.

Liz got to her feet and put on her jacket. "Have you forgotten you were a Montague and I was the closest thing to a Capulet?"

He put his hat on. "I haven't forgotten anything about that nightmarish situation."

"But it's over now." They left the restaurant and headed for the truck. "Do you want to know something Sadie told me? It's very sad."

"I'm all ears."

"When she was writing the obituary on Daniel for the paper, she said she almost wrote, 'Ding-dong, the wicked witch is dead.' Her own father…"

They'd reached the passenger door side. He looked down at her. "That's tragic."

"Isn't it?" Her eyes had filled with sorrow. She climbed in the cab. He walked around and got behind the wheel to start the engine.

"Thank God everything came right in the end. My brother would never have come back to life otherwise. Sadie's his whole world. Always was." They took off and headed for the RV park, where he'd made reservations.

"All the time she was in California she was in mourning for Jarod. I think she sobbed through half our phone conversations over those years. Theirs is a great love."

Connor supposed that if he envied his brother anything, it was that. Connor hadn't been so lucky and had missed the mark. He and Reva had been a mismatch. He knew it as surely as he was sitting there, and nothing would ever change it. "I guess you know that since Sadie's successful heart operation they're trying for a baby. She doesn't keep anything from you."

"There are a few things, I'm sure." Liz's eyes closed tightly. "Oh, I hope they get pregnant soon. That nursery they built in their new house needs a little body in it."

"I have a feeling Grandpa is going to hang on until it happens. He can't wait!"

"I can't, either. Mom and I are crazy about Sadie's half brother, Ryan. Can you imagine having two little angels to squeeze and love?"

Connor had been in an emotional abyss for a long time. But looking over at the radiant face turned to him, he could imagine it and a lot of other things. Before he did something that would shock her senseless and get them in an accident he said, "Let's go take care of *our* lovebirds."

"Good idea."

Once they'd parked for the night, she entered the trailer and grabbed two bananas. "They love these, skins and all."

He grinned. "I prefer my Snickers."

"I've found that out."

They walked back to the end of the trailer. "I'm sure

they can hear us talking," she said before going inside. When they led the horses out of their stalls, Sunflower nibbled her with affection, causing her to laugh gently. Connor wouldn't mind doing that to her himself, but he'd have to wait until the time was right.

"How's my buddy?" He rubbed Firebrand's forelock before giving him a banana.

His horse snarfed it down. When he looked over, he could see Sunflower was making short work of her treat. They walked their horses away. Then an amazing thing happened. Firebrand moved next to Sunflower, who rested her head on his neck.

"Do you see what I'm seeing?" Liz whispered.

"I bet you can't wait to get this down for your article."

"I'm going to title it 'Lovebirds at the Arena.'"

He threw back his head and laughed into the air. It was a mild winter night in St. George. There was no snow here and it was pleasant beyond words. Then his cell phone rang again. The horses' ears pricked in response. He was sure Liz's did, too, but he let it go on ringing.

A half hour later they'd put their horses to bed for the night and could go themselves. His phone rang again as they entered the trailer. Liz turned to him. "Whoever is trying to get you isn't going to go away until you answer. I'll shower first to give you privacy."

He didn't need privacy. Once she'd disappeared in the bathroom, he listened to his voice mail. Reva was at the hotel waiting for him.

He texted her that he wasn't in Las Vegas. When he arrived tomorrow, he'd call her at the hotel.

By now he should be feeling some rush of excitement at the thought of seeing her again, but nothing could be further from the truth. He resented her intrusive phone calls. Something had been happening to him since Liz had agreed to come to Las Vegas with him. Tonight he felt as though he'd been spirited away to a different place and point in time with nothing to do with his past life.

Concern for his grandfather prompted him to phone the older man he loved. He wondered how Ned's visit had gone. Once he got him on the line, Connor told him about the horses and Liz's speculation about them experiencing romantic love.

"That girl's a horse whisperer. If anyone can figure it out, she can."

"Well, so far they're acting sweet on each other. Now, tell me about Ned. Did you see him?"

"No. He went straight to his parents' house and spent time with the family. Your great-uncle Tyson called me and told me what went on. It wasn't good. They've got Ned on a medication that has calmed him down, but he's not himself and very quiet. He's going to need a lot of therapy, but at least he was able to come home for a first visit."

"That's something. As you've always told me, time is the great healer."

"Yup. How's that working out for you?"

When he looked around, Liz was just coming out of the bathroom in a different pair of pajamas, this time in a green print. In a moment of gut honesty Connor answered, "It's working, Grandpa."

It's working.

Chapter Four

Before Liz went to bed, she reached into her purse and wrote out a check. After signing it, she handed it to Connor, who was sitting at the kitchen table with the phone still in his hand.

He glanced at it. "What's this?"

"Before you give me trouble, I want you to know I already added the word *generous* to that list I'm keeping on you. You wouldn't know how to be anything else, but I wouldn't have accepted your offer to ride with you if I couldn't reimburse you every few days for my expenses."

She saw him hesitate before he folded the check and put it in his shirt pocket. "Thank you."

"I'm the one thanking *you* for not giving me a hard time about it. I like to pay my own way as much as possible." She walked over to the sofa and pulled out the bed. Once she got in, she finished braiding her hair. "How's Ralph tonight?"

"Good. Ned came for a visit."

"Did he see him?"

"No. He spent all his time with his parents. It's too soon for anything else."

"At least the doctor said he could visit them. That sounds like progress to me."

"Maybe." He got to his feet. "I'll grab my shower now."

"I tried to leave you plenty of hot water."

He stopped at the door to the bathroom. "Like I said earlier, you're too nice."

Liz frowned. He'd said that before in so many words. His words struck her like a backhanded compliment. He'd been in a relaxed mood until now. While she'd been showering, he'd had time to make other calls. Something had upset him. She didn't think it had anything to do with Ned.

After finishing her hair, she reached for the phone to call her parents. She told her dad what Connor had said about waxed reins. He told her Connor had a point and she should try the knotted kind when she practiced. See which one she liked better, since it was a personal preference. Maybe it would make a difference to her, maybe not.

They chatted a few more minutes before she hung up and returned Doc Rafferty's call. He wanted to talk about a difficult case.

"Thank goodness everything turned out all right in the end, Sam. Talk to you soon."

Connor had just come back in the room in a pair of gray sweats. "Was that Dr. Rafferty?"

"Yes. He thought he would lose a cow giving birth today. She had a closed uterus, but he got the farmer to help him roll her to untwist it. Then they had to wait for her to dilate. When that didn't happen, he had to perform a Cesarean in the freezing cold. But the little heifer is fine and so is mom. I should have been there to help."

"You can't do it all, not when you're on your way to winning a world championship."

"The way you talk, you make me think it's possible. I wish I could work the same magic on you."

He turned off the lights and climbed into the niche in one easy movement. "Why do you say that?"

"Because there's something disturbing you. If my desire to pay you back offended you in some way, we need to talk about it."

She heard a sigh. "You're way off base, Liz."

"Good. Since my check wasn't the reason, I can go to sleep with a clear conscience for tonight."

"A clear conscience. What would that be like...?"

"I said *for tonight*. You think I don't have demons driving me mad, too?"

"Name one."

"Out of which group?"

He looked down over the edge at her. "You mean you put them in groups like animal, vegetable and mineral?"

"No. My demons fall into other categories altogether. There's the bad, the awful and then the downright ugly."

Connor's rich male laughter rang throughout the trailer.

"Judging by your mood on the way to the bathroom, I'd guess tonight's demon has you rattled, but since you can still laugh, I'd only put it in the bad category."

He lay back down. "I have a dilemma, but it could involve you, so I'm going to tell you what has me worried."

"Go ahead." Connor had her full attention.

"Though we've talked on the phone a few times, I've only seen my ex-wife twice since our divorce two years ago. Last evening she phoned and left a message that she was coming to Las Vegas for a few days hoping to see me. She'll be staying at a hotel and is there now."

Liz cringed. "I see." Like she'd told her mother, Connor was still in love with his ex-wife and she with him.

"She knows the RV park where I always stay. Because she's a journalist and very tenacious, there are times when Reva doesn't care about crossing boundaries. She might show up at the trailer trying to find me. While we're in Las Vegas, the truck and the trailer are yours as much as mine. I just wanted you to be prepared ahead of time for any surprises."

"Thanks for the heads-up."

"I didn't know she was going to do this, Liz. I swear it."

"It's none of my business, but in case you're worried, I believe you."

"Thanks for being understanding."

"I'm glad you told me." She didn't need to ask him if he was all right. Hearing from his ex-wife had rattled him. "Since you're probably wide-awake now, do you want me to turn on the TV for you?"

"Thanks, but no."

On impulse she said, "Want to play a little five-card stud? I brought a couple of decks with me. I don't know about you, but cards have a way of settling me down when I've got stuff on my mind."

He'd reached the floor before she could blink and

turned the lights back on. "You're exactly what the doctor ordered." Excitement lit up his brown eyes.

Pleased by that positive reaction, Liz reached into her suitcase for the cards and walked over to the table. "That's because I *am* the doctor. Here. Take this pill. It will help." She threw him a Kit Kat bar.

Connor let out a happy yelp before they both sat down and started playing. After a dozen rounds they turned to Pineapple and then Crazy Pineapple, both variations of Texas Hold'em poker.

"You're good at this."

"Same to you. If nothing else, waiting around for a rodeo event to start has produced a ton of crack poker players. We could be dealers in Las Vegas after we're through with the rodeo."

Connor squinted at her. "Does your daddy know about this surprising side of his daughter?"

"Between my parents and your grandparents, who do you think taught me and Sadie how to play in the first place?"

He sat back so the front legs of the chair were off the floor. "I didn't know that. We'll have to get up a game after we're back from finals."

"Then you're asking for it," she teased to contain the rush his suggestion produced. "Sadie told me she outbluffs Jarod all the time."

He sat forward. "I have news for you. He lets her win to keep her happy, except when it comes to his favorite poker game."

The way he was staring at her brought out the heat to prickle her face. She put her hands palm down on the table. "Speaking as your doctor, I can see our card game has put you in a better frame of mind. We both ought to be able to sleep now."

Connor's grin was wicked. "You keep thinking that, sweetheart."

That image of him stayed with her long after she'd scuttled back to bed and put the covers over her head.

Soon it was dark and quiet. Her thoughts turned to the woman who still anchored for a television show out of Los Angeles. Did his good-looking ex-wife still go by the name Mrs. Bannock when she wasn't in front of the camera?

Liz knew nothing about her and had formed no opinion of her. Liz had been away at vet school during that year he'd been married. As she'd told him earlier, she'd had no clue that he'd gotten a divorce until months after the fact.

But tonight she decided Reva Stevens had a fundamental selfish streak. Even if they still loved each other, it was cruel to call Connor with the kind of news she'd sprung on him right before his first round of competition to win a sixth world title.

That insensitivity proved to Liz that his ex-wife didn't value his former achievements or what he was hoping to achieve now. Otherwise, she wouldn't have dared interfere with his concentration.

According to Connor, his ex didn't recognize boundaries if she wanted something. It sounded as if she wanted him back. Liz had no way of knowing if Connor wanted the same thing.

But couldn't Reva have waited until the pro rodeo finals were over? Ten crucial days out of his life to accomplish what no other bulldogger had done before? Liz decided his ex-wife didn't deserve Connor.

But in all fairness, Liz couldn't rule out physical attraction and chemistry, those potent forces a person might wish to escape because of other problems, but couldn't. Was that the case with Connor and his ex-wife?

In turmoil, she turned over on her back.

Before you start finding fault with Reva, better take a good look at yourself first, Liz Henson.

A LATE-MORNING SKY of high wispy clouds over Las Vegas greeted them as Connor pulled into the RV equestrian park at eleven. The temperature registered fifty-nine and was climbing.

This was his fourth year bringing Firebrand. To make things more familiar, every year he reserved the same spot closest to the arena and barn, and the same stall, in order to cut down on any tension for his horse.

Luckily the manager of the park had arranged to get him the stall next to Firebrand, as well. The surroundings might be new to Sunflower, but she'd grown used to being around Firebrand. As long as they weren't separated, both ought to do fine.

After he turned off the ignition, it occurred to him he hadn't awakened this morning with that sense of dread over the unknown that was coming once the finals were over. He could blame this elevated change in his mood on the attractive woman seated next to him.

He turned to her. "Shall we exercise the horses first?" To his amusement, she asked him the same question at the same time. They both chuckled before Liz jumped down from the cab first to walk back to the end of the trailer. In the side-view mirror he admired the way her feminine figure moved until she was out of sight.

He shoved on his cowboy hat, thinking this had all been too easy. Something was wrong for everything to have gone so smoothly this far. But as Connor got out of the truck, he realized that if there was a problem, it was because he was looking for one. It had become a pattern of his.

The other morning, after they'd stopped to visit his grandfather, Liz had picked right up on it and had gotten after him for it. That was the moment she'd come alive, treating him to a fiery side of her nature he hadn't witnessed before.

Last night he'd tensed up before telling her about Reva. But whatever reaction he'd feared, Liz didn't even blink. Instead, she'd made the rest of the night so much fun, he hadn't wanted to go to bed.

He rebelled at the idea that their road journey down here was over. The only thing helping him was the fact that they'd be living together for the next twelve days, and then there'd be the trip back to Montana. Though they'd been neighbors all their lives, he'd only started getting to know her on this trip. Connor was already looking forward to the drive home with her.

Together they backed their horses out of the trailer and took them on a walk before heading for the barn. With the finals starting on the fifth, the place was packed. Some of the competitors stayed here with their rigs. When they recognized Connor they shouted to him and tipped their hats to Liz.

The two of them led their horses into the barn and found their stalls. Connor emptied some bags of soft shavings around both stalls.

"This is really a nice setup, Connor. Every facility we need is here!"

"On the fourth we'll trailer the horses to the rodeo grounds and stall them there if you want, but for now this is a perfect place for them."

"I agree." She patted her horse's neck. "You like it in here, don't you, Sunflower? You'll have to thank Connor for these fabulous accommodations."

"She has already nickered at me. That's all I need." He put out the buckets for water and filled the hay nets. Buckets were a good way to measure the amount of water their horses were drinking.

"They're both nickering. Did you hear that?"

Connor smiled. "Firebrand's happy they're together."

"I think they're both pleased. Come on, little lady. Let's get your boots off and give you a good rubdown. Then I've got to get over to the center and take Polly around the arena. I'm afraid she's already feeling neglected."

Liz treated her horse the way she would a child. He watched her over the partition. It was touching to see and hear how she loved Sunflower. Given this kind of treatment, that horse would do anything for her. Never in his life had he wanted anyone to win a championship more.

"When you're through over there, doc, Firebrand needs a thorough going-over, too. I think he's jealous of all the attention you're giving his girlfriend."

Her gentle laughter was like an unexpected breeze on a hot day, refreshing him.

Within a half hour they left the barn and cleaned out the stalls in his trailer. The first rule with horses was to take care of them before you did anything else. Liz understood that. They worked side by side while he unhitched the trailer from the truck.

"After we've driven to the center to check out our other horses, let's go buy you some reins. When we get back here, you can try them out. I'm curious to see if you feel any improvement with them."

"Our minds must think alike. I was just going to ask if I could take the truck later to buy some."

"Would you rather go alone?"

"No—" She sounded surprised.

"Good." He'd wanted to go with her. "I know a reputable place to get what you need."

Her eyes swept over him. "For a change, why don't you shower first?"

"Do I look that bad?"

She grinned at him. "Even in a foot of muck you couldn't look bad, and you know it, Connor Bannock."

He swept his hat off his head. "Well, thank you, ma'am. That's the sweetest sweet talk I ever heard."

"Well, don't get too used to it. Your head's going to swell right up after your next championship. You'll be too heavy for Firebrand to prance around the arena with you in front of your thousands of screaming fans."

Connor's heart came close to palpitating out of his chest. "Are you a psychic, too?"

She shook her head. "Nope. I've been studying the statistics on you. Barring a catastrophic force of nature, you're favored to win. Nothing would make me or your parents happier. I'm sure they'll be looking down at you."

"How did they get into this conversation?"

"Once, when Ralph was giving me and Sadie some

barrel-racing pointers, they both came out to the pad-
dock. They'd been watching you practice at the arena
with Wade. We heard your dad say that no one worked
harder than you, whether it was ranch work or training
for the rodeo. They both said they were so proud of you
they could burst. Of course Ralph agreed."

A lump as large as a boulder lodged in his throat.
"It's kind of scary how well you know what went on
at the ranch behind my back."

"We weren't there all that often, but I'll tell you
this. Everything I heard about you would make you
happy inside."

"You've forgotten Ned."

"I'm trying to, but there you go again, determined
to stomp all over yourself. Those Corriente bulls from
Mexico that you throw around have nothing on you."

He laughed before hurrying to get cleaned up. Come
to think of it, he'd been doing a lot of laughing since
they'd driven away from the ranch.

Once he'd showered and dressed in a clean shirt and
jeans, he made them bologna-and-cheese sandwiches
along with a fresh pot of coffee. "Nice," he remarked
when she joined him a few minutes later smelling like a
meadow of spring wildflowers. She was wearing jeans
and a red-and-blue-plaid hombre shirt with horn snaps.

"Thanks."

He gave her another sideways glance. "It's a good
thing I'm going out shopping with you. I'm afraid you
won't be safe in those duds on your own."

"Throwing more bull, Bannock?"

"Just stating the truth, ma'am." He wondered how
she'd react if he told her she was a knockout in that
outfit.

She gave him the once-over out of dark-fringed green eyes. "That shade of brown suits you."

"And here I was afraid you wouldn't notice."

Her arched brows lifted. "You'd be surprised what I notice. Thanks for the lunch. I'll be out in the truck when you're ready to go."

LIZ COULD TELL Polly was happy to see her. She kept nickering. They took a walk around the arena to help her get used to new surroundings, then Liz stalled her again. "I'll be back later, I promise."

She gave the horse an apple, one of Polly's favorite treats, and then she left the tent area to meet Connor at the truck parked out in back. She'd been to Las Vegas several times with her parents, but for short periods. With the horrendous traffic, she was glad Connor knew his way around town. It gave her a chance to look at everything.

The marquees were dotted with the names of famous cowboys, cowgirls and celebrities who'd flocked here to enjoy the festivities of rodeo at its best. Entertainers were hosting special concerts at various venues across the city.

"Did I tell you I've seen half a dozen marquees so far with the name Connor Bannock up in giant letters? You own this city."

"Me and a hundred others," he mumbled, but she heard him. "Just remember one thing. Here today, gone tomorrow."

"This is your sixth year of being on top. That's not peanuts, as my father says. Seriously, Connor. You've honored me by asking me to drive here with you. It's a thrill of a lifetime, one I'll never forget."

When his hand reached out to squeeze hers, she almost had a heart attack. "I have news for you," he said. "Your company has been a bonus in ways I hadn't anticipated." He held on until he found a parking space in front of a local tack shop and had to let go. But his warmth continued to flow through her like sun-kissed Montana wild honey when you could find it out riding.

As they got out of the truck and entered the store, several wolf whistles reached their ears. Connor flashed her a speaking glance. "See what I mean? You need protecting."

You walked right into this, Liz. When he's back with his wife, you're going to pay for it.

She might have known Connor would be friends with the owner. He came out of his office, and after introductions were made he gave them the red-carpet treatment. Before they left with the reins Connor specified, the owner wished them luck and took pictures of them.

"This bulldogger here is the greatest of all time," he said, clapping Connor on the shoulder.

Liz nodded. "I already know that. We've been neighbors from the time we were born. I watched him growing up. No one could beat him, and no one will beat him this year, either!"

Another shocking thing happened when Connor put an arm around her shoulders and pulled her against him. "Mark my words, Stan. This year Liz will take the championship in barrel racing."

The older man smiled. "I'll be there in the front row, watching."

She eased away from Connor and hurried out of the store. It was one thing for him to grasp her hand in the truck from a surfeit of emotion to do with his parents. That, she understood. But the feel of his arm around her shoulders was something else.

He'd been paying her a supreme compliment in an effort to make her feel good, of course. To be held by Connor for a brief moment didn't mean anything to him and shouldn't mean anything to her. She needed to get over it. It was the unexpectedness of his doing it in front of someone else that had thrown her.

On the way back to the arena, they stopped to fill up with gas. Connor looked at her. "I want some gum. Can I get you anything while I'm in there?"

"Not for me, thanks."

"Be right back."

While he was inside the crowded station, her cell rang. When she saw the caller ID she felt a stab of guilt before clicking on. "Kyle?

"Hey, you—are you in Vegas yet? I thought I'd have heard from you by now."

She shut her eyes tightly. In truth, she'd forgotten all about him. "Sorry. I got in late last night and have been out shopping for some gear for my horse. I was going to call you this evening. Where are you?"

"Yellowstone. I had a delivery here and will be flying home in another hour, so I thought I'd try to reach you now."

"I'm glad you did."

"Are you nervous? Excited?"

"Both," she said as Connor got back in the cab and started the engine.

"I'll bet. I'm looking forward to next weekend. I've got three days off so I can enjoy the rodeo and spend some time with you after you've won the championship."

"Don't I hope," she said as they drove away. Liz might not be able to spend much time with Kyle after the rodeo if Connor wanted to get right back to the ranch.

"There's no doubt in my mind you'll win."

"Thanks for your support. It means a lot. Now, I'm afraid I have to hang up and start putting my horse through our routine. I don't want her to think I've deserted her."

"I think I'm jealous."

"Don't be. After Las Vegas, my barrel-racing days are over."

"Forgive me if I tell you I'm going to be glad you'll have more time for us. When is the best time to phone you?"

"Maybe it would be better if I call you."

"I'll be waiting. I miss you."

"Me, too." She wished it were the truth. "Thanks for the call. Take care flying back."

"Always."

No sooner had she hung up than Connor said, "Which one of your favorites was that?"

"Kyle."

"Where is back?"

"The airport in Bozeman. He's an air-cargo pilot."

"I presume he'll be coming to watch you compete."

"Yes."

"When?"

"On the last night."

"Has he ever seen you in action?"

She took a deep breath. "Not yet."

"He'll be blown away by the good doctor."

"You're good for my ego."

"Then we're even."

Connor...

He drove to their spot in the RV park. "Leave everything else in the truck and I'll lock it. First person to reach their horse gets a free Milky Way."

"You're on!" A good race was exactly what she needed to expend her nervous energy.

The two of them took off running. She was fast, but no match for him. They whipped past other people. When she tried to enter the barn, he turned around in front of her, preventing her from reaching the stalls.

"Connor—" She was out of breath. "You're cheating!"

"Is that what I'm doing?" He blocked every advance she made. There was fire in his eyes. Her pulse raced off the charts. "Sorry, sweetheart, but no Milky Way for you." He'd backed up to her stall.

"You're the one who's going to be sorry for this. I'll get you when you're not expecting it."

His smile was wicked. "Before or after midnight?"

"Maybe while you're mucking out the stall."

"Whoa. Just remember you'll be in there with me." She laughed. "You're shameless."

"I'm not the one with the halo."

Was he trying to rile her with comments like that? Daring her to do something outrageous? While she was trying to figure him out, he went into Firebrand's stall. In a minute they walked their horses out of the barn to the trailer where they saddled up and put the new reins on Sunflower. Liz had no idea if she would like them or not.

"Let's find out how those work for you." Connor brought along her bagged set of barrels. Once they'd mounted, they rode around the park several times and finally headed to the arena. Some riders were there for pleasure; others were putting in practice sessions before the first night of rodeo events coming up day after tomorrow. Competitors would be out here every day from sunup to sundown to get in the needed workouts.

"I'll set these up for you."

"No, Connor. You need to practice."

"Wade will be over later and we'll work out then. Right now I want to help you."

"I didn't expect this."

"Well, you've got me, little princess, so use me!"

"Little princess—?"

"That's what Grandpa calls you behind your back."

"You're kidding!"

"I know a few things you don't know."

"I'm sure you do," she muttered. She was touched that he would share something that personal with her. "Thank you for your help."

"That's better. This is fun."

He was like a kid out there setting up the four red, white and blue pop-ups with weighted bottoms. After placing them in a diamond pattern, he got back on Firebrand to watch her from a distance. "Are you ready?"

"Yes!" Her heart raced because it was Connor watching her every move with his expert eye. She wanted to put on a good show in front of him.

"Let's go, Sunflower. Easy at first." She took off to do her ten-minute trot-and-lope drill around the barrels. At first, the new reins were a distraction, and she told Connor her horse could tell.

"Keep sticking with it, then give her a rest and come back this evening to try again. If they still don't suit you, then forget using them. The last thing I want you to do is lose your concentration because of them."

Good advice.

"You're looking great out there."

Sunflower seemed happy to be put through her paces after traveling in the trailer for such a long time. By now, they'd acquired a fair amount of bystanders watching them, but if she'd developed nerves, Connor was the source of them.

The king of the cowboys was taking his precious time to help her be the best she could be. Short of winning his love, which she could never have, she was the luckiest woman in the world to be sharing this special moment in her life with him. Liz wouldn't have missed this experience for anything on earth.

She leaned forward and patted the horse's neck. "Good work, Sunflower. We'll come out again later."

Connor gathered up the barrels and put them in the bag before they rode back to the trailer to remove all the gear. With that accomplished, they walked their horses to the barn and mucked out the stalls. A lot of nickering went on.

"It sounds like they're having quite a talk," Connor murmured.

"I know. Maybe Sunflower is confiding in him."

"Stop worrying about it, Liz. I could kick myself for suggesting you might like these reins. If I've thrown you off, I'll never forgive myself."

"Of course you haven't!" she cried softly. "I'm a big girl. I didn't have to buy them, and I plan on trying them again. You feel too much guilt over problems that don't exist."

"Is that what I do?"

"Yes. It makes you a very nice person, but a troubled one when you don't have to be. Let's go back to the trailer and I'll fix us some sloppy joes and salad."

"That sounds like heaven."

Once they reached it and went inside, Connor washed up in the bathroom while she washed her hands in the kitchen. As Liz got the hamburger out of the freezer to thaw in the microwave, she heard a knock on the door. A special knock. It was probably Wade.

She walked over to open it. There stood Reva Stevens in a fire-engine-red two-piece suit and heels. Her makeup was perfect.

Thank heaven Connor had warned Liz.

His ex-wife was a stunning woman with black hair that flowed to her shoulders and light blue eyes. She was beautiful and petite, standing shorter than Liz by several inches.

"I'm looking for Connor Bannock. This is his trailer, isn't it?"

"Yes. I'm his neighbor, Liz Henson."

"Oh…from Montana. You and Sadie are good friends."

"Yes. And you're Reva. Since Connor and I are both competing in the rodeo, he was kind enough to trailer my horse with his."

"Is Wade with you?"

"No. He came in his own trailer with his girlfriend. Connor and I just got back from the arena. He'll be out of the bathroom in a minute. Please come in."

"Thank you."

Liz went back to the kitchen area. At a glance, she could just imagine what Reva was thinking. The signs of two people living in close quarters were all over the place. If Liz were in Reva's shoes right now, she'd be having a major meltdown.

"Hey, little princess— later on tonight I want a re-match of Pineapple."

Reva had just sat down on the sofa when Connor emerged from the bathroom. At his announcement, Liz watched his ex-wife spring back to her feet.

Chapter Five

Connor hadn't had time to phone Reva yet. She looked gorgeous, as usual. He'd be a liar if he didn't admit to certain emotions flooding his system at the sight of her. Moving closer, he kissed her cheek. "It's been a long time."

"Too long," she whispered.

"I can see you've met Liz Henson."

"Yes." But her eyes continued to search his. "I've been waiting for your call."

"I was just going to phone you. We had to exercise the horses first."

"Understood. Can you leave now? I've got a rental car outside."

He turned to tell Liz he'd be back later, but she'd gone into the bathroom and shut the door. Frustrated, he said, "Let's go." He reached for his keys and followed Reva out the door of the trailer. She'd pulled the rental car behind it. He walked her to the driver's side to open the door for her.

She hesitated before getting in. "I know you like to drive. Do you want to?"

"No, thanks. I've been on a long road trip. You do the honors. But I don't want to go back to your hotel.

I need to put in another practice session later, so let's pick up a hamburger at the drive-through three blocks down the street to save time. We can park there while we talk."

When he got in the passenger side, she still hadn't turned on the engine. "Connor—this isn't what I had in mind when I phoned you."

He studied her for a moment. "Unfortunately, you chose the wrong time."

"If you loved me the way I love you, there'd be no wrong time."

She was right.

"I'll always love you, Reva, but we couldn't make our marriage work."

She moved closer to him and grasped his arm. He breathed in her fragrance. "Once you're through with the rodeo, we'll try again. I'll resign from my job and live with you on the ranch."

He shook his head. "After a week following our marriage, you grew so restless you couldn't get back to Los Angeles fast enough."

"That was then, Connor. I'm ready to start a family. I know it's what you want."

"Why *now?* Two years ago it wasn't what *you* wanted."

"I'm not getting any younger. A baby will change everything for me. That's why I came to Las Vegas, so I could tell you in person. I want you to think about it while you're competing. Kiss me, Connor. Please. It's been so long. Do I have to beg?"

Following her urgent cry, she threw her arms around his neck and covered his mouth with her own.

The physical side of their marriage had never been

the problem. As good as it felt to be kissing her again, something was off, but he couldn't pinpoint it right now. Out of the windshield he could see the trailer. Knowing Liz was inside, he broke off their kiss and grasped Reva's arms. She protested when he put her away from him. He could taste her lipstick.

"When the rodeo is over, I promise to contact you and we'll talk about this some more. But for now I need to concentrate, so don't phone me or come over."

Her eyes had filled with tears. "You promise?" After an extended separation, that ache in her voice had always affected him. Until now.

"I swear."

She nodded. "I know you're going to win. You always do."

"We'll see. Have a safe flight home." Avoiding another kiss from her, he opened the door and got out.

"I'll come back for the last night to watch you get that sixth world-champion gold buckle, and we'll go off together afterward for a long talk."

Already his thoughts were focused on the last night when he watched Liz take the championship. "We'll have to wait and see about that. Thanks for the support, Reva."

He closed the door and headed for the trailer. Before he reached it, he wiped any trace of lipstick off his mouth. The second he walked inside, the delicious aroma of sloppy joes wafted past him.

"You're back so soon?" Liz sat at the table eating her meal.

"Yup, and I'm starving." He put up his hand. "Don't move. I'll serve myself."

No sooner had he sat down, ready to dive in, than

there was a familiar knock on the door. "Come on in, Wade!"

His brown-haired buddy walked in. Wade was a good friend and a good hazer. They'd been working together since high school. Next to his grandfather and Jarod, Wade stood a close third in the trust department.

"Hey, Wade," Liz greeted him. "It's good to see you again."

"You, too."

"Are you hungry? There's plenty."

"It smells good, but Kim and I just finished a late lunch. Thanks anyway. After we put my horse in the barn, she took off and will come back later this evening, after Connor and I are through working out."

"I'll be finished eating in a minute." Connor glanced at Liz. "These are fantastic."

"I learned from Mom. She's never made a bad meal in her life."

"That must be one of the reasons your dad is always in a good mood."

Liz's mouth had an impish curve. "It's one of them."

Wade eyed Connor with a gleam in his eye. "Lucky man."

The green salad had a tasty dressing on it. While Connor munched, he could have added that if Millie Henson was as much fun to be around as her daughter, it was no wonder Mac Henson was a happily married man.

When he thought about it, Connor's grandparents had achieved that same kind of harmony. So had Jarod and Sadie. They'd gotten it right.

Before he couldn't mount Firebrand because he'd

eaten too much, he pushed himself away from temptation and cleared his place. "I'll do the dishes tomorrow."

"Promises, promises," she teased.

He smiled at her. "What are you going to do while we're gone?"

"I've got some housekeeping chores. Leave the clothes you want washed and I'll do them with mine. Then I'll leave for the barn and put Sunflower through another routine."

"When you're done, come on over to the chutes and livestock area. I want to know how those reins are working out for you."

"I will."

"What reins?" Wade asked when they went outside.

Connor told him, then he asked Wade, "What would you think if I started a stud farm using feral stallions?"

Wade stopped walking. He stared at Connor as if he was out of his mind. "Ferals?"

"Yeah."

"I know you're nuts about Firebrand, but you've got ferals on your mind at a time like this?"

"Why not?" Connor kept walking.

Wade hurried to keep up with him. "What's happened to you?"

"What do you mean?"

"I don't know. You seem different. Usually—"

"I'm wound up tighter than a bull on the rampage? You're right. I've been a pain for years."

"Hey, Connor—it's me. Tell me what's going on."

"I'm not sure. I'll let you know when I've figured it out."

A CROWD HAD gathered around Connor and Wade. Whether he was working with his horse or in serious competition, you knew you were watching the crème de la crème. Liz wouldn't disturb his concentration right now to talk about the reins, so she rode back to the barn to settle Sunflower for the night.

Once she'd mucked out both stalls, she went into the trailer to shower. After getting dressed, she got into Connor's truck and drove to the Vegas Style beauty salon they'd passed earlier in the day on Tropicana. It was open until midnight.

She'd been mentally preparing for this competition for years, but there was still one thing left to do that would give her a new sense of freedom. Cut her hair.

Why she hadn't done it in college, she had no idea. It was a pain to wash and braid. With a shorter hairdo she could shampoo and blow-dry it in a few minutes every night. No more braid flipping around whether she was on a horse or working at the animal hospital.

There were several clients ahead of Liz. While she waited, she thumbed through the latest magazines until she found several styles she liked. The hairdresser finally told her to walk over and sit in the chair. "What can I do for you?" she asked, putting the drape over her.

Liz showed her the pictures in the magazine.

The woman studied her for a minute before undoing the braid. "Hey, honey—you really want to cut off this hair? I know gals who'd kill for such a beautiful mane."

Liz chuckled. "I've worn it this way from childhood. It's time for a change, don't you think?"

"I don't know. It'll take a long time to grow back if you decide you don't like it."

"To be honest, that doesn't matter. After being in a

rut for so many years, I need something different." Her life was going to change whether she won the competition or not. She needed to change with it.

Her hairdresser tapped one of the pictures. "I think this cut will suit your face best and will be easy to take care of. It's a blown-out, straight variation of the layered bob with a casual sophistication. Some feathering and smooth curves that flip up give it a surprising contrast. The natural lighter streaks in your hair make it a great look for you."

"Let's do it."

An hour later, Liz used the hand mirror to inspect her hair front and back. "I love it."

The woman nodded. "I did a great job, if I do say so myself. With those bones, you're a real beauty, you know that?"

Liz flushed. No one had ever said that to her, except her dad. "Thank you."

"You could be in one of the shows around here."

Liz laughed out loud. "Not me. I'm just passing through." The hairdresser hadn't met Reva Stevens, who was a true stunner. No wonder Connor hadn't been able to resist her!

"Well, I'm glad you passed my way."

"So am I." Liz took off the drape. They went over to the counter. Liz handed over her credit card and added a tip. Already she felt lighter, as though she could fly around the arena on Sunflower.

After she left the salon, she stopped at a drugstore to buy a blow-dryer. Then she hurried back to the RV park in case Connor wanted to take the truck and be on his own for the night. No one was inside when she let herself into the trailer. He was either with Wade or his ex-wife.

The way Reva had looked at Connor earlier had broken something inside Liz. He'd been married to Reva and had loved her. His ex-wife hadn't shown up in Las Vegas for the fun of it. Though Connor flirted with Liz, and had given her compliments, she couldn't assume he'd let go of Reva completely. Liz needed to be careful that she didn't read too much into his attention to her.

With an aching heart she reached for a Kit Kat from the sack of candy, then changed into pajamas and turned on the TV to a British comedy rerun. Liz adored the snob named Hyacinth. The fabulous actress was out enjoying a riparian feast in the country with her poor, henpecked husband, Richard.

At this point in the film, Hyacinth stood on a pier, straining to hold on to the small boat carrying her husband down the river, but she couldn't last and fell into the water. It was so hilarious Liz laughed until her ribs hurt. That was when she heard a knock.

"Who is it?" she called out.

"Who do you think?" Connor's deep voice had Liz jumping off the couch.

"Just checking first."

"So was I," he answered before unlocking the door. That was the gentleman in him.

"I didn't expect you back this soon."

Instead of coming in, he stood there in his cowboy hat, staring at her through unreadable brown eyes. "I'm looking for Dr. Henson, but I seem to have the wrong trailer."

"Oh, stop it, Connor, and come in. I wish you had seen this show. It's one of my favorites."

"What is it?"

"A British comedy called *Keeping Up Appearances*."

She hurried back to the couch to finish watching, but all he did was lock the door and continue to scrutinize her from a distance. Unable to concentrate with his eyes on her, she turned off the show. "Is the change that shocking?"

Without a smile, he said, "I'm still trying to catch my breath."

"Is that good or bad?"

"Because I'm a man, it's good, but Sunflower might have trouble recognizing you."

A delicious shiver swept through her. "I'll wear my hat. She'll never notice. As for me, I won't have to fight that braid any longer. I don't want any distractions during competition."

He put his hat away and walked into the kitchen. "I could hear you laughing. For a moment I thought you must be entertaining someone."

"Only myself. Hyacinth, the woman on the show, is absolutely hysterical."

Connor smiled. "You have that amazing quality of being able to enjoy yourself no matter the circumstances. No wonder my grandfather loves having you around."

"You're full of compliments, but I sense you're a little down. Dr. Henson is in the office if there's anything you'd like to talk over."

"The fact that you're here is good enough. Let's not waste that new hairdo. How would you like to go line dancing with me tonight? I don't know about you, but it'll help me unwind."

His ex-wife's appearance had done damage. How much damage wouldn't be known until the rounds of competition started.

Liz's comment to her mom before this trip came back to bite her. *I'm thinking this will be my one and only chance to see who he really is and get over what has prevented me from moving on with another man.*

"I'd love to. Since I've already showered, I'll change out of my pajamas while you clean up."

"I guess I'd better do that if you're going to let me get close to you." A quick smile broke out before he disappeared.

Yup. That was the killer smile that had blown her away in her teens. But she was a woman now, and she'd been given glimpses of the troubled man inside his skin. Liz couldn't find the words to describe the feelings growing within her. But already she knew there was pure gold lurking inside him, shinier than all the gold buckles he'd accumulated during his life's journey this far.

She dressed in another Western shirt and jeans before putting on her suede jacket. He emerged from the bathroom wearing a new black shirt she hadn't seen. Talk about trying to catch your breath.

Her hat came last as they left the trailer for the truck. Once inside the cab he said, "This bar is in the north end. They have a great band and I like the kind of crowd it attracts. Do you mind?"

"I've been on the Strip before. Surely by now you know I trust your judgment to pick someplace different."

His gaze played over her features for a pulse-pounding moment before he started the engine and they drove out to the main street. The traffic was heavy but typical for Las Vegas. Before long, they turned off and wound around to Tiny's Bar and Grill. Though there was a crowd, they didn't have to wait to get inside.

Connor had been right about the band. It rocked. As they walked in, the people on the dance floor were doing the Watermelon Crawl. Liz found her senses throbbing to the music.

After being shown to a table where he helped remove her jacket, he ordered soda for both of them. The band was getting ready for another number. "I'm in the mood to dance."

"Me, too."

They got up and walked out to the floor. The next song turned out to be the Cowboy Boogie. The moment they started, Liz glanced sideways and saw her escort could boogie with the best of them. Many of the females in the room recognized the king of the steer wrestlers and glommed onto him in a big hurry.

Someone in the band announced that the famous Connor Bannock was in the grill. Everyone cheered. Liz loved it. He was electrifying when caught in the right mood, and he was definitely in the right mood. His eyes lit up when he realized she was well into it herself.

Liz danced her head off. She'd never had so much fun in her life. The whole crowd was living it up. Pretty soon they turned to the Sleazy Slide, and they must have danced to half a dozen songs before the band took a break.

After he cupped her elbow and led her back to their table, he leaned toward her, his eyes full of flattering male admiration. "I've never been with a woman who dances like you. Is there anything you can't do?"

If only her heart would stop its sickening thud. "I can't steer wrestle."

"I'm being serious," he ground out.

She drank her cola. "So am I. As I said before, my folks didn't get a boy."

He sipped his drink, viewing her mysteriously over the rim of his glass. "They won the jackpot."

"Try telling them that. You never heard about the pony dad paid money for that he didn't have. After I went to my first rodeo, I plagued him for one. Then I nearly drove the poor thing into the ground trying to make it go around tree stumps in the forest. I almost killed it."

Laughter started deep inside him until his whole body was shaking. It brought tears to his fabulous brown eyes. "How old were you?"

"Oh, I don't know. Maybe six. I gave them fits day in and day out for years. When I was nine, dad got me Magpie, whom I promptly crippled. After he got Dr. Rafferty to explain all the terrible things I'd done to him trying to make him run around more stumps and bumping into them accidentally, I had to nurse my horse until she was better. I think it was then I decided it might not be a bad idea to become a vet if my animals were going to survive."

A smile laced his features, giving him a dashing look. "In the midst of it all, a barrel racer was born."

"My dad was forced to train me so he would survive parenthood."

"His hard work paid off."

She averted her eyes as her throat closed up. "Let's hope so."

"You made it to the top fifteen in the world. Number two puts you in the top money earnings. As your father said, that's not peanuts." The band had started up again. "Let's dance."

It wasn't until they reached the open floor she realized the music had changed to allow everyone to slow dance. She felt a spurt of adrenaline as he pulled her into his arms and drew her close to his hard-muscled body. Their hats nudged against each other, but he didn't let that stop him from pressing his cheek to hers. She was burning up. Surely he couldn't help but notice.

When the song ended, he didn't let go. "This is nice," he whispered in a husky voice.

So nice she could hardly breathe. He continued to rock her in his arms until another song began. "I like your gold barrel racer earrings. They're unique."

"Sadie and Jarod had them made for me on the reservation to bring me luck."

"They're working so far."

Liz lost track of her surroundings. The whole time they clung to each other, his warm breath tickled the ends of her newly cut hair, sending rivulets of delight through her body. It was uncanny how they moved as one person.

"Do you have any idea how good you smell?"

"We both used the same soap, remember?"

"One of the great perks of rooming together," he teased. "I'm glad we've still got two weeks ahead of us."

And then what? Would he get back with Reva? But Liz chose not to think about that right now.

Connor lifted his head so he could look at her. "I'm waiting for you to say something back." If she wasn't mistaken, she heard a trace of vulnerability in his voice. "Have you changed your mind? Would you rather room with the other barrel racers at the hotel? It's a once-in-a-lifetime opportunity to rub shoulders with the best of them."

What to say to convince him she was happy with the decision she'd already made? "When Mom asked me why I decided to travel with you, I told her it was a once-in-a-lifetime opportunity to rub shoulders with the best of the best. That's *you,* Connor."

She heard his sharp intake of breath, which could mean anything, before he spun her around the floor. When the song ended, he grasped her hand and led her through the crowd to the exit. Silence punctuated the drive back to the RV park. By the time they reached the trailer, Liz sensed Connor had worked himself up into a mood she didn't understand.

He unlocked the door for her. "I have an errand to run. I don't know how long I'll be."

After giving Liz the thrill of her life, he was off to spend time with his ex-wife.

She knew he wasn't a player. Connor's grandfather had suggested he take Liz to Las Vegas with him. He'd probably told him to show her a good time. No one could do it better than Connor, even with Reva waiting in the wings for him.

"You don't owe me any explanation, neighbor. Thank you for a great evening out." She went inside and shut the door before locking it.

Liz checked her watch. Five after one in the morning. Too late to have a heart-to-heart with Sadie. After she got ready for bed and had crawled under the covers, she texted her best friend who would see her message in the morning.

I need to talk, but know it's impossible tonight. I'll try to reach u tomorrow. Suffice it to say, I'm in trouble.

No sooner had she pressed Send and turned out the light than her cell rang. She couldn't believe it and clicked it on. "Sadie?"

"It's not impossible because I'm wide-awake. Jarod drove to the reservation and is staying all night with his uncle Charlo's family. They're rebuilding the fence around their house. I stayed behind because I haven't felt good for the past two days."

"You're sick?"

"Yeah. Poor little Ryan doesn't understand what's wrong with me."

All of a sudden, Liz screamed with joy. "You're pregnant!"

"Yes! I just found out, but I told Jarod I was coming down with a cold because I want to surprise him when he gets back after breakfast."

"I'm so thrilled for you, I'm jumping out of my skin!"

"Me, too, but I'm *so* sick. The nausea is deadly. Still, enough talk about me. You said you're in trouble, and we both know why."

Her hand gripped the phone tighter. "I'm afraid so."

"Where's Connor?"

"With his ex-wife."

"Reva's there?"

"Yes."

"You're kidding me!" Sadie cried. "That woman refuses to leave him alone! Jarod's going to croak when he hears this."

"They're still in love, Sadie."

"So are you. I can hear it in your voice."

Liz closed her eyes tightly. "Yes. He's so wonderful, you have no idea."

"Of course I do. He's Ralph's grandson and Jarod's brother. There's no one like the Bannock brothers on this planet," she said, in so fervent a tone that Liz shivered. "I have no advice for you. Absolutely none."

"I didn't expect any. I just needed to talk."

"Go ahead and bawl your heart out. I did enough of that to you for eight years. It's my turn to listen."

The floodgates opened. "H-he's lost confidence, Sadie. It goes back a long way."

"Tell me something I don't know. I'm still working on Jarod."

Liz wiped the moisture off her face. "He feels guilty about his life."

"That sounds familiar, too. Blast Reva for showing up at a time like this."

"She can't help that she loves him."

"It's not the kind of love he needs. Jarod's worried about him retiring from the rodeo. He's vulnerable, and Reva knows it."

"I couldn't agree more."

"Thank goodness you're in Las Vegas now. How's the hotel? Are they taking special care of all you barrel racers, letting you loose in the casino?"

Guilt caused her to sit up straight up in bed. "No."

"What do you mean?"

Her pulse picked up speed. "Connor and I are sharing his trailer as our hotel while we're here."

At least a minute passed before she heard, "Liz—what's going on?"

"I'll tell you what I told Mom. After all these years of being haunted by him, he gave me an opportunity to get a real dose of him, one-on-one. I was convinced that driving to Las Vegas with him, staying with him in his trailer, would be a revelation and provide the cure I've been needing."

"Where's Wade sleeping?"

"He's driven down in his own trailer with his girlfriend."

Another silence. "My poor, dear, darling, foolish friend…"

"Sadie? You and I both know this was all Ralph's idea. He gave us this charm bracelet to hang on the truck mirror to bring us luck. Connor's trying to please him. He's been bending over backward for his wallflower neighbor."

"Wallflower—"

"The shoe fits, Sadie. I'll act grateful if it kills me."

"It's already killing you."

It was.

"You're in the worst trouble I ever heard of and the rodeo hasn't even begun yet. It beats my eight years of exile from Jarod. I thought you wanted to win the gold buckle."

"I do. Pray for me."

"I already am."

Chapter Six

Liz set her watch alarm for six-thirty in the morning. She wanted to take Sunflower on an early ride. It would give both of them a chance to work with the new reins. When she looked up, she could see Connor was in bed. He'd probably just gotten in from being with Reva and would need a ton of sleep.

After dressing quietly, she gave her hair a quick brushing. What a delight after having to take care of that long braid day after day for years! She bit into an apple, put on her hat and left the trailer. The sun was just making its appearance, a favorite time of the morning for Liz, as she headed for the barn.

When she reached the stalls, she let Sunflower finish off her fruit. Not forgetting the other horse, she slipped Firebrand a treat from her pocket. "Don't worry. Connor will be here before long."

Then she turned to her horse. "Come on, little lady. Let's give these reins another try and find out if Connor was right about them."

She led Sunflower back to the trailer. Once the mare was saddled, Liz levered herself into the seat and took off on a slow walk. Only a few people were out riding.

Slowly she ran through her routine. "Whoa," she

said every so often, pulling on the reins as Sunflower stopped and backed up. The more she worked with the reins, the more she realized she could get a good grip with those knots. The feel was definitely different.

When they returned to the arena, she started making her circles. After a little while, she increased her speed and could tell she had more control with these reins, giving her confidence. Better yet, her horse was getting the message and couldn't pull around a turn like she sometimes wanted to do because Liz had a stronger, better grip.

At the rodeo in Great Falls, Connor's eagle eye had seen the reins slide through her hands that one time. It took a champion to have noticed. Another slip like that could cost her a winning time when it came down to the wire. She owed him for helping her make a crucial adjustment in her gear.

Over and over again she practiced her circles with Sunflower, changing from a walk to a lope, one direction, then the other, then backing up. The knotted reins were what she'd needed to fine-tune her connection with Sunflower.

"By Jove, I think she's got it" came a deep, familiar male voice out of the blue.

She turned her head. "Professor Higgins!" she cried in a rush of excitement. How long had he been watching her? "You're a genius!"

"That's nice to hear first thing in the day."

Her heart melted at the sight of him astride Firebrand, his hat dipped low over his forehead to shield his eyes from the rays of the sun. In her mind, Connor had always been the ultimate American cowboy, but since their trip she'd learned he had many facets to his complex personality. He was such a marvelous man, she could hardly put her feelings into words.

"Do you want to hear something else exciting?"

A half smile broke out on his face as he rode closer. "Shoot."

"The thing we've all hoped for has happened. Sadie just found out she's pregnant, but Jarod doesn't know yet." Connor whistled. "She's going to tell him today, with a special surprise when he gets back from the reservation."

"What is it?"

"After they were married, she secretly asked Jarod's family to make her a basket cradleboard in the hope that one day they'd have a child. She has it hidden at Ralph's. I bet she ran over to get it and has put it in the middle of their bed so he'll see it first thing."

A stillness surrounded Connor. "He's going to die of joy."

"Oh, wouldn't you love to be a fly on the wall when she tells him?"

Connor let go with a whoop and tossed his hat high in the air. Pure love for his brother had inspired that maneuver. Naturally, because he was so athletic, he caught it again.

"I can't wait to hear what Crow name he comes up with after their baby is born."

He grinned. "Probably something like Howls Like a Wolf."

She laughed hilariously. "Or Bear Cub Who Makes Noise."

Connor sidled his horse right up to her. "When did you talk to her?"

"Last night, before I went to sleep. She would have

gone to the reservation with him, but felt too nauseous. I guess that's when she learned she was pregnant. The news about Sits in the Center will go out over the pow-wow drums at their next celebration," she teased. "Just think. You're going to be an uncle, and Avery will be an aunt!"

He nodded. "This will give Grandpa a reason to go on living." He smiled as he said it, but she heard a forlorn tone that crushed her, because she knew where it came from. Connor didn't feel he carried his weight as a Bannock. She couldn't bear it that he didn't know how remarkable he was.

"Ralph has three outstanding grandchildren carving out their own destinies. All of them help him get up every morning."

He studied her for a long time. "You're the one person I know who always sees the glass full. Not half-full or half-empty, but full."

"That's because it is. Have you eaten yet?"

"No. I heard you leave and decided it was my turn to muck out the stalls while you were working with Sunflower."

"That was a sneaky move on your part. You're afraid I'm going to get you when you're knee-deep in the stuff."

A chuckle escaped his throat. "The thought has crossed my mind more than once. Are you hungry?"

"I'm getting there."

"Let's drive out of town into the desert. I want to barbecue some steaks and cook up potatoes and onions. We'll take a trail ride. The horses need a break from their normal routines and it'll be fun for them. We'll come back in time for me to work out with Wade."

"Do you have a specific place in mind?"

"I thought we'd drive to Red Rock Canyon. It's not far, and there are trails running throughout with some awesome views. How does that sound?"

A whole afternoon alone with Connor now that they'd reached their destination? There had to be a reason he wanted to get completely away. *You wanted to get to know the real Connor. But you hadn't counted on his ex-wife to be a virtual presence. You are a fool, Liz Henson.*

She averted her eyes, unable to sustain his glance. "It beats spending time losing the little money I brought with me on the roulette wheel," she quipped. "Come on, Sunflower. We're very lucky our gracious next-door neighbor wants to show us something we haven't seen before. Let's see if we can't beat him and Fire-brand to the trailer."

With a clicking sound, she took off like a shot. It was exhilarating to get into a full gallop. Liz wouldn't have done it if Sunflower hadn't already been warmed up. She reached the back of the trailer first, but that was only because Connor had decided not to make it a competition. She jumped down to open the doors.

Moving quickly, she walked her horse into the stall and filled the bucket with fresh water for her. She patted her neck. "If you run that fast for me during the events, we'll have nothing to worry about."

While Connor led his horse inside the other stall, she secured the lead rope and then left the stall. Before long he'd hitched the truck to the trailer and they took off.

No one eyeing them would see a thing wrong this picture, but Liz knew it was flawed. "Connor," she began. "I—"

"Reva went back to Los Angeles yesterday," he broke in before she could apologize."

So he wasn't with her last night.

"She won't return until the last night of finals. But I want to get something clear right now. You've been more than a neighbor to me for a long time, and I'm not using you for substitute entertainment."

"I know that," she whispered. "But I guess I'm overwhelmed by your attention. When Ralph asked you to drive me here and take good care of me, I never dreamed you would be so thorough about it. It makes me feel guilty, because I've done nothing to deserve it.

"Though you warned me about Reva, when she walked in the trailer I could see what she was seeing, and it hurt me for her sake. She couldn't have been happy that I was living in there with you. If your kindness to me, or your grandfather's, has done anything to cause trouble between you and your ex-wife, I couldn't handle that. I'd be happy to explain the way things really are to her."

"Have you finished?"

She lowered her head. "Not yet. Jarod and Sadie almost didn't get back together because of horrible misunderstandings. Look at them now! If I can be of any help to you where Reva is concerned, you know I'll do whatever I can."

"Now are you through?"

"No! I'm indebted to you and Ralph for getting me here. If I accept that job on the reservation, I'll be indebted to Jarod. I guess I'm having a hard time accepting the incredible kindness you Bannocks have showered on me."

He cleared his throat. "Let's get a few things

straight. In the first place, the problems between me and Reva started a long time ago and resulted in a divorce. The fact that you're using my trailer while we're here has no bearing on my relationship with her because she and I no longer have a relationship. A miracle would have to happen for us to get together again."

Though Reva might have pursued him this time, she knew in the core of her he was still hoping for that miracle.

"Second, you're under the false impression that my grandfather asked me to drive you to finals with me. But you're wrong. He had nothing to do with it. In fact, I know it shocked him when he found out. The truth is, I allowed you to make that assumption because I was afraid you wouldn't come otherwise."

Liz knew he wasn't a liar. Her body started to tremble from those stunning revelations. "Then why *did* you ask me to come?"

"Frankly, it's because I wish it hadn't taken so long for me to get to know you, but because of Daniel I was forced to stay away. Years ago Grandpa made me promise I wouldn't go near you. That's why you and I never really connected though we've lived next door to each other our whole lives. At Daniel's funeral I was determined to fix that problem, but our schedules have been hectic.

"Last month I saw you out riding in the Pryors, working on your form. Your discipline and work ethic is absolutely phenomenal. It struck me how crazy it was that two people who love the sport like we do, and have given our lives to it, have never gotten to know each other better. That's when I got the idea to invite you to drive to Las Vegas with me. But after you turned me down in Missoula, I'll admit I was nervous to approach you again."

Her emotions were in chaos. "I can't imagine you being nervous about that."

"Are you kidding? Grandpa's little princess? Sadie's best friend? Your parents' pride and joy? Montana's wonder woman?"

"Okay, okay. Stop!" She laughed in spite of her shock.

"I didn't want to make a mistake with you. Have I made one now by asking you to spend the day with me?"

"Of course not."

"That's good. Now I'm going to stick my neck out once more and ask you another question. Have you ever wished I'd asked you to go out with me?"

With her heart slamming into her rib cage, she lifted her head and eyed him directly. "You mean before you met Reva?"

He nodded.

"Sure." She flashed him a smile. "Every girl in the county wanted a chance to be with Montana's hot steer wrestling champion."

A shadow crossed over his features. "I'm talking about your wanting to be with the second son of the rancher next door."

What did he just say?

"But now that I think about it, Bobby Felton and Ricky Jarvis always hung around you at school, so the thought to be with me probably never entered your mind."

He couldn't be serious. But when she looked into his eyes, she could see that he was. *Connor, Connor.*

The tension between them was palpable. "Do you think you can handle the truth?"

"Try me." His intensity shook her to the bone.

"The times Sadie and I went out riding and Jarod just happened to show up though it was forbidden, I always hoped his younger brother would be with him, but it never happened."

A long silence stretched between them. "When we get back from finals, plan on my showing up. If I see you with Kyle or any of your other favorites, I'll lie low until I can catch you alone."

Gasp.

"SEE YOU TOMORROW at the Mack Center, Wade. Liz and I will be taking our horses over after lunch."

He nodded. "That was a good workout tonight."

"Yup. Firebrand's never performed better."

"I'm talking about you."

"Yeah?"

"Yeah." His gaze played over Connor without saying anything more.

After Wade left the barn, Connor took care of the horses. While he made certain they were watered and fed for the night, his cell phone rang.

Jarod!

He'd been waiting for this call the whole time he and Liz had ridden in Red Rock Canyon. With certain misunderstandings cleared up, their outing had been quite perfect.

"Hey, bro—I thought you'd forgotten me. How are you and Sadie doing?" He was waiting to hear the excitement about the baby.

"I just got back from the reservation. She's so sick, she can't lift her head off the pillow."

Connor grinned. "Must be the flu. It's going around."

"It's not that. She's pregnant, and I'm terrified."

He blinked. "Those two statements don't go together. How could you possibly be terrified over news that has to have made you a new man?"

"You don't know how sick she is, Connor. I've never seen her like this in my life."

"If it's that bad, then she should be in the hospital where the doctor can reduce the nausea with medication."

"I've already talked to her OB. He'd ordered medicine for her and I just gave it to her. But what if—"

"It isn't!" Connor interrupted him. "The doctor said her heart operation fixed the problem for good. Some women get really sick. Grandpa told us our mom had terrible morning sickness for a few weeks with Avery. Remember Prince William's wife? They had to put her in the hospital for a few days. Now they have baby George. Have you got any ideas for your baby's name?"

"I can't think right now."

"I don't think I could, either, if I'd just been told I'm going to be a dad. Congratulations, bro! This is the good news we've all been waiting for."

"You really think this is going to pass?"

"I think you need a good talk with your uncle Charlo."

"He'll tell me I'm a mess."

"That's your right as a new father. Have you told Grandpa or Avery?"

"No. You're the first."

Afraid not. Liz had gotten there before anyone else. Connor loved it.

"Did you find her in bed when you got back?"

"No. I found a flat-board cradle on my side. She was in the bathroom throwing up."

Connor tried not to burst out laughing. This was one situation his big brother, who was always in control, wasn't prepared for. "I'm sorry she's sick, but you know it won't last long. Give her my love and cling to the Crow courage that led you to the light during your fast."

He thought his brother might have hung up when he suddenly said, "How are you? How's it going with Liz?"

"Sometime I'll tell you, but not tonight. Go take care of your wife. I'll call you tomorrow."

Liz was already in bed when he returned to the trailer. He looked down at her. "I just got off the phone with the father of Little Sits in the Center."

She sat up. "I love that name you made up! Is Jarod thrilled out of his mind?"

"Not yet. Sadie has bad morning sickness. He's so in love with that woman he can't handle anything being wrong with her."

"Sadie's tough."

Connor had needed to hear that himself from the one person who knew Sadie better than anyone else. "I told him we'll call him tomorrow. We'll both talk to him. Since I'm too excited to sleep yet, how about some poker after I've showered?"

"I've got another idea. Have you ever played Boggle?"

"Can't say that I have."

"I'll set it up. You're going to love it!"

He had news for her. He loved whatever he did when they were together. In truth, he didn't want the finals to end....

AFTER HER WORKOUT at the Mack Center the next day, Liz took care of her horse, then left the temporary tented barn provided for the horses and headed for Connor's rig. They'd parked on the lot of the university's soccer field. That was where she would wait for him. To her surprise, she saw a cowboy lounging against their truck with his arms folded. When he saw her coming, he waved and started walking toward her.

"Dr. Henson?"

"Oh—you're one of the famous Porter brothers I met in St. George."

"Derrick." He smiled. "I'm glad you remembered that much. I was hoping to catch up with you. Are you finished for the evening?"

"Absolutely. I put Sunflower through her paces today. We both need a rest."

"With tomorrow being our first official event, I think we've all had a tiring workout." He shoved his hat back. "I saw Connor's rig, so I'll come right out and ask if you and he are an item before I go any further."

He was nice. Rather cute. Probably her age. Maybe a little younger. "I'm his neighbor. He was kind enough to give me and my horse transportation here. I'm using his trailer as a hotel during the events."

Derrick was a friend of Wade's. It was important she made her relationship with Connor perfectly clear with Derrick because it would get back to Connor at some point.

His eyes flared in response. "One question down. One more to go. If you don't have any plans for this evening, would you care to have dinner with me?"

Though Liz was flattered by Derrick's interest in her, she didn't want to encourage him when Kyle would be coming the last night of finals. On the other hand, maybe it wouldn't hurt this one time in order to give Connor some space. He'd mentioned that they'd get together after they got back to the ranch, but she had no idea how serious he'd been about it. Since they'd left Montana, they'd been together constantly. *What to do?*

"That's okay, Liz." His smile said it was, but her lack of a quick response wasn't kind. Surely it wouldn't hurt to go with him this once. They were all competing, and he was anxious as everyone else underneath. Theirs was a unique fraternity.

"No, no. I'd like to go. It will be relaxing. The errand I'd planned to do can wait. Thanks, Derrick. Give me a minute to go inside the trailer and I'll be right back out."

"Take your time."

Once inside she freshened up and changed into a clean blouse and jeans. After brushing her hair and putting on lipstick, she wrote a message for Connor and left it on the counter.

Connor,
Have made plans for this evening. Will see you back at the RV park later tonight. Liz.

Dispensing with her cowboy hat, she walked out and locked the door. Derrick was waiting for her in his white truck. As he was helping her in the passenger side of the cab he said, "I like your new hairdo."

"I'm flattered you even noticed. Thank you."

"You're impossible not to notice, if you know what I mean." After Connor's reaction, she'd decided she should have cut her hair sooner. Derrick shut the door and walked around to get behind the wheel. "I thought we'd go for my favorite meal, if you don't have a preference."

"I'm so hungry I could eat anything."

"Even breakfast?"

"Maybe you're psychic. If I had to choose to eat the same meal every day of life, it would be bacon, eggs and cinnamon toast."

"Even if I'm not psychic, I'm superstitious and always eat breakfast the night before an event the next day."

"With two gold buckles in your possession, your system must be working. Maybe it'll work for me."

He drove them through the park to the main street. "I watched a couple of barrel racers earlier. Then I spotted you. The control over your horse is superb."

"Are you trying to sweeten me up, cowboy?" she teased.

"Nope. I call it as I see it."

"You know how to make a gal feel good."

"Just being with you makes *me* feel good."

Hopefully he said that to all the girls. Liz ended up having a nice evening. Derrick worked on his father's sheep ranch in Rock Springs and was still single and enjoying the rodeo circuit with his brother. They mostly talked shop.

At ten-thirty they drove into the RV park. Connor

had brought his rig back from the center. The truck was there, too. He might be inside or with Wade, but it didn't matter. Just the thought of him sent a minor quake through her body.

"Tomorrow night a few of us are going to attend a party at the Bellagio, but we'll go to the South Point Hotel first to see the gold buckles given out." She knew all about the Wrangler NFR–hosted event. It was held in the ballroom of the main casino every night. "Would you like to go with me?"

She was ready for him this time. "I can't make plans that far ahead. Why don't we wait until tomorrow night to see what it brings?"

"Fair enough. I'll look for you after your event is over."

Liz gave a nod without actually committing herself. "Good luck to you and your brother."

"The same to you. See you tomorrow night."

Maybe, but she wouldn't be going out with him again. "Thanks for dinner. Don't get out." She opened the door and jumped down.

Liz felt his gaze on her as she approached the trailer and reached inside her purse for the keys. But before she could get it in the lock, Connor opened the door.

"Hey, Connor." With a smile, Derrick waved his hat to him before driving off.

There was no answering smile from her host. He locked the door behind her, looking the way her father had in her teens when he didn't know where she'd been and was worried. But her heart knocked against her ribs over the lack of animation on his face. "Is Sadie worse?"

For a few seconds he didn't say anything.

"Connor?"

"Sorry. What did you ask?"

"You look so upset, I thought you must have had bad news about Sadie."

"I'm sure she's all right or I would have heard from Jarod," he mumbled.

"Then what's wrong?"

He shot her a piercing glance. "Derrick's a player. I thought you'd already figured that out."

Was Connor jealous? Was it possible? She sat down in one of the chairs. "It was just one dinner with another competitor to talk shop."

"So *that's* what you were doing?"

"He approached me at the rodeo grounds and I didn't want to be rude, knowing he's a friend of Wade's and a little uptight waiting for tomorrow." It was the truth.

"Wade said he has a girlfriend back in Rock Springs, but I wager Derrick didn't mention her." His brows lifted. "Has he asked you out again?"

"For tomorrow night, but I told him I couldn't make plans."

"That was smart."

She couldn't believe this had come out of him. For Connor to be upset over Derrick thrilled her to the heels of her cowboy boots.

"I don't know what will happen in my event," she said. "But I want to see you get your buckle. For five seasons in a row you've had the winning time the first night of every competition. It's unheard of. That's why you're a legend already."

No compliment could nudge him out of his foul mood.

"Connor? Have you eaten yet?"

"No." He rubbed the back of his neck. "I wasn't hungry."

"Ah. So this is what happens to you the night before an event. You need food. That's why you're a grump. I'll fix you some eggs. They taste good anytime."

She put her purse on the couch and got out the eggs and bacon from the fridge. In a jiffy she found the frying pan and started cooking.

He stood there, watching her, with his hands on his hips. "What did you have for dinner?"

"Breakfast."

"He took you to breakfast?" The scowl on his face spoke volumes.

"It's my favorite meal."

"I know." His head reared. "Did you tell *him* that?"

She was beginning to believe Connor really *was* jealous.

"Only after he told me it was what he wanted for dinner. Why don't you sit down?" She made coffee and set a place for him. Pretty soon she'd served him breakfast and added some of the toasted English muffins he liked.

To her satisfaction he ate every bite.

"That was delicious. Thank you. Wade wanted me to go eat with them, but I didn't feel like it. When I got back here, I didn't feel like cooking, and I apologize for my behavior."

"The king of the steer wrestlers has every right to experience an off night."

"*You* never have one."

"Don't worry. My turn is coming, so be warned."

When he'd finished, she cleared his place. Then she

took some thin chocolate after-dinner mints out of her purse and put them in front of him.

"Where did these come from?"

"The restaurant. I thought you'd like them with your coffee."

"So you *were* thinking about me." He sounded happy about that.

"Of course. Since you and I left the ranch, it feels like we've been joined at the hip. I thought you might like a breather, but you knew I'd be back. I didn't want to return empty-handed."

It seemed those were the magic words. On that note, he undid the foil wrappers and gobbled the mint down, causing her to chuckle. "You remind me of Sunflower enjoying her favorite treat."

The light had come back into those dark brown eyes. "I like treats."

She smiled. "I know."

"If ever you feel like giving me more, make them chocolate."

"I know your tastes by now." Liz cleaned up the kitchen. Connor obviously wasn't up to partying. He'd done all those things with Reva once upon a time. She couldn't blame him for brooding over his situation now. "How did your workout go?" she asked over her shoulder. "Feel like you're ready?"

"I never feel ready," he muttered.

She leaned against the counter. "Neither do I. I'm so glad you admitted it first. Maybe you'll think this sounds crazy, but I feel at a loose end without Sunflower tonight. She's in a new place. Even with Polly there, I'm sure she's missing me and Firebrand. The barrel horses are in a different row inside the barn."

"Tell you what. Tomorrow night we'll bring them both back to the RV park and give them a shampooing. Might as well keep them here for the rest of the competition. It will be much quieter and friendlier for them."

"That would be wonderful," she blurted.

"You never wanted to move them there, did you?"

"I didn't know."

"Well, we know now." He got up from the table. "I'm glad there's a smile on your face. In the meantime, will *I* do for company?"

She turned away from him. "Always." The word slipped out before she could prevent it.

"Want to go for a swim? The indoor pool is open all night."

She'd forgotten there was a pool. "That'll be the perfect place to unwind. I'll change into my suit."

After finding it in the bottom of the suitcase, she hurried into the bathroom to change. Then she put her clothes on over it and grabbed a towel. Connor carried his suit and towel with him. They left the trailer and made their way to the building that housed the pool. Several guys were in the shallow end, talking along the edge.

When Connor left to change, she removed her clothes and got in at the deep end. Two men promptly swam over to her, forcing her to tread water. She figured they couldn't be a day over nineteen.

"You're that barrel racer we've seen out in the arena with Connor Bannock."

He had fans everywhere. "That's right. Are you two here to compete?"

"Don't I wish," one guy said. "I'm Bart. We're students at the university, but love the rodeo."

"Ah."

"We both work here during the day," the other guy said. "I'm Casey. We found out he was registered here and hoped to meet him and get his autograph. I saw you working with him earlier. You're a sensational rider, too."

"Thank you."

"Since you're friends with him, what do you think? He's so famous that after he wins his sixth gold buckle, we won't be able to get near him."

"I'm sure he'll give you one. Have you got something for him to write on?"

"Be right back!" They both charged out of the pool and disappeared.

"What was that all about?" Connor had plunged into the pool and emerged at the deep end next to her. The water made his hair look darker, giving him a different look she couldn't resist.

"Two fans who work here at the RV park and are dying for your John Henry. I told them you'd do it. Do you mind? You're their idol."

The way he appraised her sent licks of flame through her body. "As long as that was all they wanted."

They did some laps together, taking their time to reach the other end. Before long, the two guys came back to the pool carrying the things they wanted autographed. Liz turned her head toward Connor, who'd edged up close to her. His closeness caused her heart to thud.

"Go ahead and make their night with that thousand-dollar signature, cowboy."

"Come again?"

"That's what it will be going for down the road."

She stayed in the water while Connor bounded to the patio and talked to them for a minute. They were all smiles as he signed what looked like a poster and a magazine. Before they left she heard them call out, "Thanks, Dr. Henson. We didn't know you're competing, too. We'll be cheering for you tomorrow night, as well."

Curious how Connor always referred to her as *doctor* in front of other people.

"Thank you!" Liz waved while she waited for Connor to get back into the water. That was when the idea to "get him" took root. As he swam up to her, she did a strong kick, splashing him in the face, something he wasn't expecting.

He sputtered for a second. "So you want to play?"

"Better here than giving you a muck bath in the stall."

In a lightning move he caught her ankles and pulled her to the center of the pool, where he swung her around with her arms flailing, making her dizzy. "Connor—" she shrieked in laughter, helpless to defend herself. "Stop!"

He kept going. "Had enough?" His devilish smile shook her to the foundations.

"Yes—"

Connor towed her to the shallow end and sat down on the step, where he pulled her onto his lap so she sat across with his arms around her. His eyes bored into hers. "You always seemed so untouchable to me. For years I've wanted to get close to you like this, to find out if you're really real. It's been such a long wait, don't deny me what I want right now. I couldn't take it."

She heard his ragged voice implore her before his

mouth covered hers. A moan escaped her lips. Surely this wasn't happening. The urgency of his kiss caught her off guard. He'd stolen her heart years ago, but right this minute he'd stolen her breath.

Mindless from the sensations he was arousing, let alone the warning bells, she forgot everything except her hunger for him. This incredible man was kissing her as if he really meant it. As for Liz, she *did* mean it with every fiber of her being and was letting him know.

When his hands roved over her back, drawing her closer still, she realized what she was allowing to happen. Afraid of her needs spiraling out of control, she wrenched her mouth from his.

"No more, Connor—" She refused to look at him. "I've crossed a line I swore I wouldn't do this trip. It's my fault, not yours." She tried to get away, but he wouldn't let her.

"Now look who's apologizing. Fault doesn't come into it. I caught this enchanting mermaid in an aqua bikini swimming in my territory. What else is a man to do?"

"Or a woman," she admitted. "But since we've had our fun, let's quit while we're ahead. Believe me when I tell you you're the best of the best, whether rodeo champion or second son of a rancher. It's my privilege to know you and be your friend. But tomorrow the competition begins in earnest for the last time in our lives. I don't want to do anything that distracts us from realizing our dreams. I know you don't, either."

She slid away and dashed up the step to the changing room off the patio. Her hands shook as she removed her suit and got dressed in her clothes. Sharing accommodations had made this moment inevitable.

Connor was waiting for her when she stepped outside the building. The temperature had dropped. They hurried toward the trailer in the distance.

"If you think I'm sorry for what happened back there, you'd be wrong."

Liz darted him a smile. *Keep it light.* "I enjoyed it, too." The unimaginable had happened and she was still reeling.

"Good. When we get back to the ranch, we'll pick up where we left off."

But with Reva waiting for his rodeo career to come to an end, was he trying to convince Liz or himself? Was that what his kiss in the pool was all about? "By the time we get back to Montana, the focus of our lives will have completely changed."

"Thanks to you, mine already has."

Her pulse sped up. "In what way?

"A feral stud farm. The possibility has taken hold of my mind. If I were to undertake a venture of that magnitude, I'd need a vet I could trust with my life. Would you be interested?"

She swallowed hard. His ex-wife was coming to Las Vegas on the last night. Liz was afraid of what it meant. To work with Connor for the rest of her life while the happily remarried couple lived next door?

Liz's conversation with her mother came forcefully to mind.

I'm convinced that driving to Las Vegas with him will be a revelation and provide the cure I've been needing.

And if it isn't?

If it isn't, then I'll have to take a serious look at my life and make changes.

That's what has me worried. Bannocks never pull up roots. That means you'll be the one who'll end up moving somewhere else.

A shudder swept through Liz as they entered the trailer. Millie Henson's words might just have turned out to be prophetic.

"That would mean stretching my practice in too many ways, but I'm flattered you would even consider me."

"At least promise me you'll think about it."

There was no reason to give him a flat-out no yet, not when he was actually considering her idea for using ferals. If anyone could do it, *he* could. "Let's get through the competition first."

"Agreed. Do you want to shower first?"

"Do you mind? Then I'll blow-dry my hair while you're in the bathroom. It's so noisy, it will keep you awake otherwise."

She grabbed a clean pair of pajamas and hurried into the bathroom. But after she'd closed the door, she sank down onto the floor and slumped over her raised knees for a minute while she tried to recover.

Love's first kiss.

Any other kisses before this didn't count.

She'd read about it in the fairy tales. Now she understood why it had brought Snow White violently awake. Prince Charming's passion had created a bonfire. Liz was burning up.

Chapter Seven

The day of the first round of the pro finals was upon them. "What do you think I should wear for the opening ceremonies?" While Liz cooked eggs and ham, Connor held up two Western shirts, one black, one brown.

She glanced at them. "Black will make a big statement."

"Black it is. Why don't you wear the royal-blue shirt I saw you hang up in the wardrobe? When we parade in front of the crowd with the other competitors from our state, every eye will be focused on you."

"You're throwing bull again." But her pulse throbbed from his compliment. Liz couldn't believe she was actually going to be a legitimate competitor in front of thousands of people at the Super Bowl of rodeos with Connor. Everything was starting to feel surreal.

"What? No argument?" he teased.

"Not today."

"Well, that was easy."

She chuckled. "Come and eat. I've made French toast, too."

"I love being spoiled rotten."

Liz loved being with him, period!

After breakfast, they cleaned the trailer, washed sheets and made beds. Then came the phone calls to and from family and friends. She received a text from Kyle wishing her luck. She sent him a message back with a thank-you. Keeping busy was the best way to handle the countdown.

At 11:00 a.m. Connor drove Liz to the South Point hotel to attend the Women's Pro Rodeo Star Celebration. There was a banquet program where they were handed out gift packs of an NFR ring, a jacket and a backpack. The finalists drew for the saddles.

Wade carried hers and put it in the back of the truck, then they headed out into the desert.

Later in the day, Connor fixed them lunch. After eating, they drove back to the trailer to shower and get ready. Once they'd reached the Center, Connor reached for the silver charm bracelet.

While he held on to one end, he motioned for her to catch hold of the other, their link to Ralph. "Shall we have a moment of silence?"

"Yes," she whispered, moved by his suggestion. Since driving with him, she wanted the best for him, not only for the rodeo, but for his very life.

He squeezed her hand before rehanging the bracelet around the mirror. She felt his warmth steal through her. "After our events, I'll wait for you here and we'll drive over to the South Point together. Later we'll load up the horses and take them back to the RV park." He leaned across the seat and kissed her cheek. "My bet's on you, Liz."

"I think you know how much I want you to win."

Within the next hour it was time to get in line for the parade. She'd watched it on TV for years. Incredible to think she was finally a participant. After the presentation of the American flag and the national anthem, there was the laser light and fireworks show.

It thrilled Liz to be riding alongside Connor. When their horses nickered back and forth, Connor flashed her a smile that turned her bones to liquid. He leaned closer to her. "They know something big is about to happen."

She nodded. "Sunflower is excited. I can tell."

"Firebrand has more nervous energy than usual, too." In the background, the music blared. "It's time," he said in his vibrant voice. "Ready?"

Liz heard the announcer introduce the contestants from each of the twelve pro circuit regions. A thunderous ovation greeted their ears when she and Connor rode out of the alley into the spotlight.

"From the State of Montana, give a huge welcome to Connor Bannock from White Lodge, unprecedented five-time world-champion steer wrestler hoping for his sixth on his champion horse, Firebrand. This triple-crown winner two years in a row has raised the bar."

The crowd went absolutely crazy with applause and cheers, raising the noise level. Liz heard thousands of people chanting Connor's name. She was so proud of him she could burst.

"New to this arena, also from White Lodge, is Liz Henson, number two in the standings of the world barrel-racing championship, riding Sunflower. When she's not competing, she's known as Dr. Elizabeth Henson, veterinarian." More cheers and whistles erupted. Sunflower fairly pranced. Sometimes she almost seemed human.

"Next is Pete Marshall from Ennis, sixth in the

world standing in tie-down roping on his horse, Foxy. This is his third appearance at the finals. Finally, let's greet Greg Pearson from Gardiner, number ten in the world standings in bull riding. This is his fourth appearance at this arena." The applause continued before they exited the stage and the competitors from the Prairie Circuit made their entrance.

Liz followed Connor to Firebrand's stall. His event would be coming up soon. "I'll leave you and Wade to get ready. Go for it, Connor. Go all the way."

His eyes searched hers. "I'll find you after my event is over to cheer you on. There's no one who's better at what you do than you. Just remember that, and forget everyone else. This is your time."

Those words sustained her as she put Sunflower in her stall. Anxious not to miss anything, she made her way through the crowds to get the best view of the steer wrestlers. They were walking their horses in preparation for their event. She watched Connor from a distance talking with Wade, no doubt assessing the steers for tonight.

When it was time for the steer wrestling, she moved to a spot by some of the rodeo livestock support staff. This was the first night of the competition, which meant Connor, who was number one, came last.

The first twelve bulldoggers clocked times from 3.6 to 4.2. She heard Shorty Windom's name announced. The Floridian put a 3.5 on the board. "That's the winning time so far!"

It was a terrific score.

"Next up is Clive Masters, number three in the winnings from Amarillo, Texas." He took off and was fast, tying with Sonny Anza from Ojai, California, for a 3.6.

The crowd grew louder as the Arkansas champion Jocko Mendez's name was announced. Number two in the winnings, he was Connor's competition. Liz's heart began to thud as she watched him take off, but he went too fast.

"Uh-oh. Hitting that barrier too soon wasn't in Jocko's plans for this first round. That'll cost him, but he could still be number one if his overall average beats everyone else's."

Seconds later she saw Connor enter the box. "Can the number-one–ranked, five-time world champion bulldogger, Connor Bannock, from White Lodge, Montana, beat the best time tonight?" A roar broke from the crowd in answer.

Her breath caught in her throat.

"He's in the corner of the box, scoring his champion horse, Firebrand. Will his luck hold? For five years he's had the winning time on the first night of the pro final rounds. We'll see if he can do it again."

Just do your best, Connor, because you are the best.

She watched him give the nod, and before she could blink, he was out of there, going thirty miles an hour. Moments later, he had that steer on the ground in a flawless performance. "Ladies and gentlemen—he's broken his own record with a 3.2! Your winner for tonight, Connor Bannock."

The crowd went crazy with excitement, but no one knew what his win meant to Liz. *Now maybe you'll believe in yourself, Connor.*

She turned around and headed for the stall to brush down Sunflower and talk to her. When it drew close to the time for her event, she resaddled her, put on the knotted reins and her show bridle using the O-ring snaffle.

Once in the saddle, she leaned over and patted her neck. "Okay, little lady. We're being televised. This is it. What do you say we do this for my mom and dad? Without them, this night would never have been possible. Let's do it for Ralph who always believed me, and let's do it for Connor. He got us here safe and sound."

Liz headed toward the alley where the other barrel racers were assembling. She waited before getting into line, since she wouldn't go until second to last. His words echoed through her mind. *There's no one who's better at what you do than you. Just remember that and forget everyone else.*

Taking his advice, she forced a calm to come over her and went through a series of mental calisthenics. Sunflower did a few sidesteps, knowing what was about to happen. She was so smart it was scary.

At the precise moment it was her turn, Liz made the clicking sound her horse recognized. They shot down the alley. This was a blind barrel. You couldn't see it until you came out into the arena. To Liz's relief, Sunflower rated perfectly at the first barrel, the way they'd been practicing, and they raced across the arena to the second barrel. Around they went. Her horse had never made a better turn. Now the last barrel! *Don't knock it over.*

Once they got around it, they needed to fly back to the alley, and fly they did. Like the wind! She heard the announcer give her time as 13.61. That was the best time she'd ever had! The crowd went wild.

"Good girl, Sunflower. You outdid yourself!"

Trembling with excitement, she walked the horse

back to her stall. Everyone called out, "Great ride," and congratulated her before she reached her destination and dismounted.

"I love you, little lady," she said, hugging her while tears ran down her cheeks. She pulled a treat out of her pocket and gave it to her. "I have the best horse in the world."

"That works both ways" came the deep masculine voice she loved behind her. "Sunflower has the best rider in the world. It's over. You won tonight's round and the competition is in mourning. Dustine, who's number one along with three others, knocked over barrels. She did an 18.90. All Las Vegas is betting on you to win the world championship."

She wheeled around, the moisture still glistening on her face. "*Connor*—you won, too!" she cried. "I'm so happy for you I could—"

"Burst?" he finished for her. "Congratulations." He reached for her and hugged her. "Tonight beats every rodeo experience I ever had. We should have been traveling to all our rodeos together."

Liz's father had told her he thought she and Connor were the best kind of company for each other.

"Hey, Liz—how about letting another cowboy give you a hug? That was a dynamite performance."

She could see Derrick over Connor's broad shoulder and eased away from him, though he seemed reluctant to let her go. "I'm sorry I wasn't able to watch your event. How did you do?"

"Not as good as you and the legend here." He smiled and nudged Connor's shoulder. "Sixth-best time for me and my bro isn't great, but we'll try to recoup tomorrow night."

"You have nine more tries," she said in an effort to prop him up.

Derrick smiled at her. "Are you ready to claim your gold buckle? I'll drive you to the hotel."

She wished he hadn't sought her out, wished she hadn't gone to dinner with him. Now he'd shown up at the wrong moment. Liz wanted to stay in Connor's arms indefinitely.

"You go on." Connor answered for her, but the light had gone out of his eyes. "I'll head over to the hotel in my truck to join Wade and my sponsors. See you there."

CONNOR HAD FELT euphoric until Derrick had shown up. *Hell.* When Connor had hugged Liz just now, she'd clung to him in a way that sent a shock wave through him. More than her win—or his—had caused a reaction like that. He could feel something profound happening to both of them. He couldn't be wrong about that, could he?

On the drive over to the hotel he received a text on his cell. He pulled it out. Way to go, lover. 9 more days. Can't wait.

He put his phone back in his pocket. At five to eleven he showed up at the casino where Wade and their road buddies were waiting for him. The Wrangler NFR announcer began the presentations. There was tons of laughter and a few tear-jerking moments as he and Liz picked up their buckles along with the other night's winners.

Connor got as close to Liz as he could. They exchanged an intense glance before they had to leave the stage so the main concert could begin. He could feel that she'd wanted to be with him. While the fans started to two-step the night away, he watched her join Derrick, who was eating her up with his eyes.

When they disappeared, he said good-night to Wade and Kim and headed back to the RV park to hook up the trailer. En route Jarod phoned to congratulate him.

"Sadie and I invited the Hensons and Zane to watch the whole thing on our big screen with Grandpa and Avery. Neither you nor Liz could do anything wrong. You know that?"

"Liz's performance was phenomenal."

"So was yours, bro."

"I got lucky. Jocko had a bad break. That was tough."

"He was too eager to beat you."

"He still could."

"But he won't! You should have seen our grand-father. He and Millie just sat there crying like babies from the moment of the opening ceremonies. When Liz's score flashed on the screen, Mac lost it. I never saw him break down before."

"I'm not surprised. She rode for him. Before we hang up, tell me how the mother of Little Sits in the Center is doing."

Jarod chuckled. "So-so. The medicine is helping, but she's in for a siege of morning sickness, I'm afraid."

"But nothing you can't live with."

"No, thank heaven. We'll all be watching again to-morrow night. Sadie's here with me. She sends her love to both of you."

"Tell her thanks. I'll let Liz know."

"You mean she's not with you?"

He bit down so hard he almost cracked his teeth. "Afraid not. She's…partying."

"Liz?"

Connor shouldn't have said anything. "I didn't mean it that way. In truth, I have no idea what she's doing with Derrick."

"Who is that?"

"The guy in the team roping with his brother. He's a friend of Wade's."

"Does that mean Reva's there with you?" he asked in a quiet voice. "Grandpa told us she called the house before you left. What's up?"

He sucked in his breath. "She wants to get back with me."

"As in married?"

"Yup."

"Are you with her right now?"

"She came for a night, but I sent her back to L.A. We'll talk when the rodeo's over."

After a silence, "Have you figured out what your heart's telling you yet?"

"Yeah," he said without hesitation. *Oh, yeah.* "Thanks for the call, Jarod. Tell Grandpa I'll phone him in the morning."

"Will do. I have no doubts tomorrow night will bring another top score for you. But if you're not happy with it, remember I'll always be proud of my brother. Take care."

"You, too." They clicked off. Connor was glad he had work to keep him from going crazy until Liz got home.

Another hour and he had the horses put to bed in the barn at the RV park, safe and sound, as Liz put it. He showered and got ready for bed. After he'd climbed into the niche he heard the key in the lock and felt his pulse pick up speed. When she came inside, Connor sat up.

"Welcome home."

Her head jerked around in his direction. "Hi!"

"I thought you wouldn't be in for hours."

"I'm not interested in Derrick and told him I wanted to get back to the trailer. No partying for me while I'm here."

At that news Connor's foul mood did a complete reversal. "Did he ask you out again?"

"He tried, but I told him I needed all my wits about me to concentrate on the rest of the competition. When he asked me to go out with him on the last night, I told him I already had plans with the man I've been seeing."

"You mean Kyle."

"Yes."

He released the breath he'd been holding. If she was in love with Kyle, she wouldn't have agreed to drive with Connor. "How did that go over with him?"

"Not well. He said he's not giving up."

"He's a player. By the end of the rodeo he'll have found someone else."

"I hope. Partying takes too much energy out of me. I don't know how everybody else does it."

"Not everyone won the gold buckle tonight, that's why."

After hanging up her jacket, she took the box with the buckle out of her purse and put it on top of his box sitting on the table.

"That's quite a centerpiece, Dr. Henson."

"If you perform the way you did tonight, that pile is going to grow, Connor Bannock."

"Shall we make a pact to win eighteen more and build a skyscraper?"

She flashed him a brilliant smile. "Why not? The dream to make it to the Dodge Ram and Wrangler Finals has come true for me. Now I have one buckle. Who says there aren't more to be won?"

With a mysterious look in her eye, she reached into her purse and tossed him what looked like an oversize silver dollar. "After your fabulous performance I knew you'd be waiting for your treat, so I asked Derrick to stop at the Quick Mart."

On another burst of adrenaline he unwrapped it and bit into the chocolate. His eyebrows lifted. "You know you're stacking up points with me, right?"

"I hope so. I'm so deep in your debt already, I'll never climb out."

Good. That's where I want you.

DERRICK THE PLAYER was in for a huge disappointment, Connor mused, and smiled secretly as he lay back against the pillows. He listened while she showered. Soon she emerged from the bathroom and turned out the light before getting into the pullout bed. "Does Kyle have a truck and trailer?"

"Why do you ask?"

"So he can drive you and Sunflower home. That's what he intends to do, right? But if he doesn't have the equipment, I'll be happy to trailer the horses back with me. Then you and Kyle can do what you want."

"Thank you for being your generous self," she said in a subdued tone of voice. "But to be honest, I haven't made plans that far ahead yet."

"Maybe he's planning to surprise you and fly you home in his plane."

"Whatever the case, it's not your concern. You have your own plans to work out."

With a frown, he moved over to the edge to look down at her. "Why do you say that?"

"Didn't you tell me your ex-wife would be coming the last night? You may not want to go right back to Montana after finals are over. Fortunately, you and I both have enough of a support group that we don't have to worry about our horses getting transported back home. In the meantime, all I want to do is concentrate on getting through the next nine nights. Now, if you don't mind, I'm exhausted and need to go to sleep."

On impulse he said, "You sound a little out of sorts."

"I'm sorry. I told you I have a bad night now and then. Forgive me?"

"You ask that after what you've had to put up with me? Want to talk about it?"

"No, thank you."

"Plan to sleep in. I'll take care of the horses in the morning and fix us a big breakfast. When you're up, we'll take them for a ride. How does that sound?"

"Wonderful." When he thought there wasn't any more, she said, "Connor?"

"Hmm?"

"You're too good to be true."

"No one ever said that to me before." It was the truth.

"If they didn't, they *thought* it."

Liz's mood was different tonight. Something was bothering her. Too many guys on her plate wanting her? He recalled an earlier conversation with her.

Who's the lucky guy in your life?
Dad says they're all lucky.
All? Why aren't you with your favorite?
They're all my favorites for different reasons.

Connor pounded his pillow, but no matter how many times he did it, he couldn't get comfortable. Hell, hell and hell.

Chapter Eight

On the seventh day of competition, Liz discovered they were running low on food again. For the past six days they'd enjoyed eating all their meals in the trailer between training sessions and doing laps in the swimming pool.

"Connor? Do you mind if I take the truck for a little while?" He'd just awakened. His tousled dark blond hair made him so handsome, she had trouble not staring at him.

"What's up?"

"We need groceries. I'm going to run to the market so we can fix breakfast. Later on we'll exercise the horses."

"I'll go with you."

"But you don't have to."

He smiled. "What if I want to?"

"After winning another buckle last night, you deserve a long sleep in." Three more boxes had been added to their centerpiece. Since the first night, Connor had won two more buckles and Liz had won her second.

Both of them were still among the top three finishers on the other nights, but the competition was tight and fierce. Jocko Mendez had copped two buckles since his disastrous first night. As for Dustine Hoffman, Liz's competition, she'd also won two buckles.

He jumped down from the niche. "I'm up."

"Once we leave the trailer, you run the risk of being besieged by your fans."

"If you'll protect me from the females, I'll ride flank to protect you from all your new ardent male admirers."

"You don't ever run out of that sweet talk, do you, Connor?"

"You bring it out in me, sweetheart."

Never in her wildest dreams had she imagined going grocery shopping with him. When they reached the supermarket, he grabbed a cart and they walked up and down the aisles together, choosing the items they wanted. His jokes provoked constant laughter from her. Shoppers could be forgiven for thinking they were romantically involved. If Liz wasn't careful, she'd start to believe it.

Living together in semiseclusion had been working for them so far. By avoiding other people and the distractions of Las Vegas itself, they'd achieved an easy relationship and a schedule that was good for them and their horses. But in four more days this artificial world they'd created for themselves would end.

When she and Connor got back to the trailer to put the groceries away, nothing could have upset her more than to read Kyle's text. He'd made arrangements to stay at the Luxor and had already purchased his ticket to watch the events on her last night of competition. He was prepared to rent a truck and horse trailer to drive her home—whatever she wanted.

No. She didn't want him to come. From the second

she'd driven away from the ranch with Connor, the idea that, in time, she might grow to love the pilot had shriveled. It didn't matter that Connor and Reva might be getting back together for good. Liz knew it was no use to go on seeing Kyle.

Until she found a man she could love with the intensity she loved her next-door neighbor, it wasn't fair to mislead Kyle or any other man. Her dilemma was so severe, she needed to talk it over with Sadie before she answered his text.

After she'd fixed a late breakfast for them, Wade came over so he and Connor could put in another practice session. Liz begged off, saying she had some washing to do but would join them in a little while. For once she was relieved to find herself alone, and immediately phoned her friend.

"Sadie?"

"Liz! I've wanted to call, but was afraid it wouldn't be the right time."

"You never have to worry about that. How are you feeling?"

"Well enough with the medicine I'm taking, but forget me. Your scores are fabulous. You keep this up and your average will mean you come out the winner."

"So far, my luck is holding."

"It's more than luck. Jarod says you'll win the whole thing."

"What did he do? Consult his uncle Charlo?" she teased.

"He doesn't need to. It's in Jarod's blood to have visions, too. He's had one about you, but told me I couldn't tell you."

Liz didn't know whether to laugh or faint. "Did he have a vision about his brother?"

"I asked him the same thing. He said no."

The way Sadie spoke sent a chill through Liz.

"I still have no advice for you about Connor."

"He and Reva will be getting together after finals, but he's not the reason why I'm calling." Connor had been having fun with Liz, saying and doing all the right things to make her feel good and desirable. She'd felt his passion, but their time together was almost up. "This is about Kyle." She explained what was wrong. "If you were in my shoes, what would you do?" The silence went on for a long time. "Sadie?"

Her friend finally let out a sigh. "Since you didn't want Kyle to drive with you to Las Vegas, I think you should tell him the truth. That this isn't the time for you to get together with him. Surely if you explain about family coming and your responsibility to Connor and the horses, he'll understand, even if he's disappointed.

"Tell him you'd love to go out with him after you're home. By then, all the stress of the rodeo will be over and you can find out if the two of you have a relationship worth pursuing. Maybe, when you see him after being with Connor, you'll be pleasantly surprised. Maybe not. In any event, it'll be easier to say goodbye to Kyle knowing you didn't let him spend all that time and money to come be with you."

"Agreed." It was the advice she needed, because she'd been thinking with her hormones. "You're right. Thanks for being the best friend I ever had."

"Ditto."

"Give Ralph my love."

"You know I will. We'll all be watching again tonight. Go knock 'em dead!"

After they hung up Liz made her daily call to her mom, who sounded happy. Whatever worry her parents might have because of her feelings for Connor, they could see her scores had never been better. *Connor had been good for her.* It was the rest of her life she had to worry about, but she refused to think of anything but finals right now.

Her next call wasn't going to be so easy, but she had to do it. Kyle was a great guy who'd been trying to make plans with her. Maybe he would never want to see her again, but she knew herself too well. Better to disappoint him now than to pretend to be happy to see him after he flew in to Las Vegas. She couldn't do that to him, not when she felt the way she did about Connor.

She answered his text with another one, asking if she could phone him in an hour about something very important. He said he'd be available in a half hour.

Once she put the phone away, she headed over to the barn and put Sunflower through a special routine to keep strengthening her hocks. Those precision turns required the greatest power and discipline from her horse. During the workout, Kyle called her back.

He was mostly silent after her explanation, but incredibly decent about it. She promised him she'd drive to Bozeman to see him as soon as she got back from Las Vegas. That was, if he wanted her to come. To her surprise, he assured her he would look forward to seeing her.

Why couldn't she be in love with him?

After lunch, Connor watched while she got out her doctor bag and gave both horses a thorough medical exam. Liz had been doing this every other day. So far, her check for soft-tissue injuries, as well as hoof and teeth problems, had turned up nothing. Their horses' hearts and lungs, their breathing and digestive noises sounded normal.

She nodded to Connor. "They're in excellent shape. We've been lucky so far."

"Thanks to you. I've never traveled with a vet before. Like I said earlier, if it hadn't been for Daniel, we could have been doing this from the time you graduated from med school."

Yup. That would have been about the time he got his divorce. But with his career in rodeo over in the next four days, it looked as though Connor would be getting a second chance to make his former marriage work.

She looked into his eyes. "I wonder how many times Jarod and Sadie have said those same words."

He rubbed the back of his neck. "They went through hell. We all did, but that time is behind us," he ground out. "What do you say we drive our children over to the center and put night number seven behind us?"

"I can't believe we're getting near the end."

"I know what you mean: Our horses are lucky. They don't think the way we do and have no idea when this whole business is going to end. Until it's over, they just keep going."

"That's what we've got to do. Just keep going for four more nights." Liz leaned over to pick up her medical bag. Her breath caught when she felt his hands slide up her arms to her shoulders. He squeezed them gently. His warm breath tickled her neck. "You're going to win. I feel it in my bones."

Jarod had predicted a win for her, but not for his

brother. That alarmed her in the most profound way. She wished Sadie hadn't said anything, and turned to Connor so he'd let go of her. Liz couldn't handle his touch right now.

"I've already won by making it to the finals and traveling here with you. So far, the two buckles are simply a bonus."

His expression sobered. "I don't think you know how good you really are." He always managed to say the right thing at the right time, denoting a selfless, generous nature she admired so much there were no words.

"I was just going to say the same thing to you." With her medical bag in one hand, she caught hold of Sunflower's reins with the other and started walking toward the parked trailer.

"Hey—what's the hurry?"

"I want to walk Sunflower around and hang out by the alley without feeling the stress so she doesn't build up too much tension about it. Then I have to leave for the Las Vegas Convention Center. Wrangler has set up my autograph time for six-thirty. I wasn't allowed to pick it. Unfortunately, it means I probably won't get back in time to watch your event."

He grinned. "If you've seen it once, you're not missing anything."

"Don't be absurd, Connor. No one knows how hard you work to get each ride perfect. Thank goodness I only have to do this once."

"You have no vanity."

Fire shot from her eyes. "I've got plenty, but not during *your* event! Promise you'll phone me after you've finished and let me know how you did."

THREE HOURS LATER, Liz's words still resounded in Connor's heart as he backed Firebrand into the corner of the box for his turn. On his right he caught sight of Wade mounted on his horse on the other side of the chute. He sent Connor a speaking glance, letting him know this steer was a wily one. It looked to be six hundred pounds or better. Connor had seen them all, from four hundred and fifty to six hundred and fifty pounds.

With an answering glance he acknowledged Wade's message, then patted Firebrand's neck. "This is it, buddy."

Connor gave the official nod and the steer shot out, releasing the rope barrier. Firebrand took off. Connor rode low and leaned to the right, sliding down his horse to hook his right arm around the steer's right horn. With his left hand he grasped the left horn to slow it down and braced himself with his feet. His body knew these maneuvers like the back of his hand.

But the steer unexpectedly bucked upward as Connor threw him to the ground, resulting in a sudden, powerful load on his chest muscle. It sent excruciating pain shooting through his chest and shoulder before running down his right arm.

In a flash he knew he'd sustained a serious injury.

Just like that, *he was finished.*

The shock of the physical pain was bad enough. But the knowledge that the end of his career had been cut short four days early by an accident tore through his gut as if he'd been ripped open by one of those horns.

While the arena workers took care of the steer, the emergency staff came running to carry him out of the arena on a stretcher. Only the announcer's voice commiserating over the injury sounded in the eerie quiet of the crowd who were on their feet waiting to know the outcome. Everything was surreal. He saw Wade's ashen face loom over him.

"Don't worry. I'll take care of Firebrand," he assured Connor.

"I know you will. Wade—" It was hard to breathe. "Wrangler set up a schedule for Fan Fest. Liz took the truck and is at the convention center right now signing autographs. Find her when she gets back here. She'll have heard about the accident, so help her. She *has* to place again tonight. Do you hear me?" Connor muttered through clenched teeth.

"I'll do whatever I can," Wade promised before Connor was carted away in an ambulance. Once he'd been lifted inside, the last thing he remembered was someone sticking him with a needle.

WITH HER AUTOGRAPH session finished, Liz pulled up in the parking area at the back of the Mack Center. Before she got out, she heard her cell ring. That was the call she'd been waiting for. Excited, she pulled the phone out of her purse. But her spirits plunged when she saw Derrick's name on the caller ID. What on earth was he doing phoning her? She'd made it clear she didn't want to see him again.

A strange feeling crept over her before she clicked on. "Derrick?"

"Liz? I just saw what happened to Connor and I can't tell you how sorry I am."

A cold, clammy sensation broke out on her skin. "What *did* happen?"

"Oh, hell—you don't know?"

"Know what?" Her voice shook.

"He got injured during his event and was taken to the hospital."

Her eyes shut tightly. "How badly was he hurt?"

"I don't know. I thought you—"

"I've got to go."

Blind with pain, she rummaged for her keys to drive to the nearest hospital, but suddenly her door was flung open. It was Wade. He reached in and put his arms around her.

She lifted tear-filled eyes to him. "Derrick just told me the news. Is Connor going to live, Wade?"

"Sure he is. He injured his chest and shoulder, but he'll be fine."

"Is that the truth?"

"I wouldn't lie to you about this."

"Oh, thank God," she whispered before slumping against him. "I've got to go to him as soon as I finish my round."

"While he was on the stretcher, he begged me to find you and make sure you won your event tonight. I promised him I'd follow through. Just sit there for a few minutes till the shock wears off."

"So he was coherent the whole time?"

"Yes."

"What went wrong?"

"The steer was as ornery as they come. As Connor was throwing him, it bucked upward, probably causing a torn muscle."

Liz moaned. "He must be in so much pain."

"Even so, he was worried about you. I'll go to the hospital with you after your event. I can promise that the only news he'll want to hear is that you placed in tonight's event or won it. That'll help him get better in a big hurry."

She couldn't bear it. That sixth gold buckle had been denied Connor. Her heart broke for him. "His family has to be devastated after watching what happened on television." Ralph would need a lot of support. He loved Connor so much.

"Connor has a great family who are there for him all the way and will help him get through this. He's survived many injuries on the circuit."

"But this finals was his last." Her voice broke.

"I know," he said quietly.

"It's so cruel. He's the best and would have won the whole thing."

"I'm convinced of it."

She sniffed. "But five world championships isn't bad, right?"

He smiled. "Right. Do you think you've recovered enough to go inside and get ready? I'll stay right with you."

"I'm thankful you're here, Wade. What I want to know is, are you all right? This has to have been heartbreaking for you, too. Connor couldn't have made it this far all these years without your help. He has sung your praises over and over again."

"That's nice to hear. I'll be fine. You know this business better than anyone. There's always a risk."

She nodded and wiped her eyes. "I'm feeling better and should get ready."

"Let's go."

Liz had found her legs and headed inside for Sunflower's stall. She knew how much Connor wanted her to win. Tonight she'd do her very best to keep the rodeo alive for him until it was over.

While Wade chatted quietly with some of the other contestants around her, she comforted herself with the thought that Reva would have heard about his accident by now. No doubt she'd be on a plane to Las Vegas before morning. It would thrill him to see her walk into his hospital room.

With his career over, he could concentrate on a new life with Reva that would bring him joy and, later on, a family like the one Jarod and Sadie had started.

"Okay, little lady." She spoke to Sunflower before mounting her. "Our turn is coming up. We've got to do this one for Connor."

Wade gave her a private nod before she walked her horse toward the spot where the barrel racers had started to congregate. She noticed several competitors were having trouble with their horses not wanting to enter the arena.

The swell of cheers from the crowd signaled that the first racer had finished her run. Liz watched the second racer gallop down the alley for her run. The audience roared with excitement. Sunflower sensed their turn was coming and took a few steps in anticipation, but they'd be racing next to last.

When Liz finally heard her name announced, she made her clicking sound and they bolted out of the alley into the arena. Her horse knew the cloverleaf pattern they'd done hundreds of times and did it to perfection. They skimmed the third barrel but incurred no penalty. Then they went flat out for home. She heard a time of 13.47 announced. Her best one, giving her a third gold buckle.

Overjoyed, she cried, "Good girl, Sunflower!"

Wade was waiting at her stall with a beaming face. "You did it again!"

"Thanks."

She dismounted quickly. No matter how big a hurry she was in to see Connor, she had to drive to the South Point for the awards and then return to take care of her wonderful horse. She gave her the attention she needed plus a special treat, then she moved over to Polly's stall and talked to her for a minute, also giving her a treat.

Wade joined her. "Follow me to the hospital in Connor's truck. Let's exchange phone numbers in order to stay in close touch."

"I was just going to suggest it."

With that done, the trip was a complete blur to Liz. Her heart rate was too high to be healthy, but it wouldn't return to normal until she'd seen Connor for herself and knew he really would be all right in time.

He had a private room on the third floor. The nurse at the station told them he was only allowed one visitor at a time. Apparently it had been like Grand Central Station, and their famous patient needed rest. He'd be undergoing surgery at 6:00 a.m.

"You go in first, Liz."

She bit her lip before letting herself inside.

Naturally he'd been given painkillers, and he lay there, still and pale beneath his tan. But when she approached the side of the bed, his eyes opened. Their beautiful brown color hadn't changed.

"You got a 13.47," he murmured.

"Yeah. How about that?" She pulled a chair up close to him.

"Where's my treat?"

"I'm a doctor, remember? You can't have food before surgery. Love that outfit you're wearing, by the way. Picked it up at the Western store, did you?"

His lips twitched. "I talked to everyone at home. By now they know you're a shoo-in for the world championship."

She fought the tears prickling her eyelids. "So tell me the bad news."

"The doctor is going to repair my pecta something."

"Ah. You've suffered from a violent eccentric contraction of the pectoralis major muscle that caused a rupture at the humeral insertion of your right arm. That's not surprising, since you used that arm to catch the horn of that blasted steer. According to Wade, it was an ornery critter."

His eyes smiled. "How did you get so smart?"

"It runs in the family."

"You're not kidding. Liz—" She could see his throat working.

"Don't say it. I don't want to hear it. Five world championships are more than any human has the right to expect in this life. You're already a legend. The steer caused all the trouble, not you, Connor Bannock. Tonight you went out in a blaze of glory no one will ever forget, so enjoy the downtime.

"This hospital will have to be cordoned off to protect you from thousands of fans dying to know how you are. Since you're much too modest, I'll set up a blog to let everyone know that their hero is alive and kicking. I'll even put up some pictures of before and after. You owe it to them."

"You'd do that for me?"

"After all you've done for me, I don't know how

you can even ask me that question. It'll be a good way to advertise your feral stud farm if you decide that's something you want to do. Now I'm going to leave so Wade—"

"Don't go—I don't want to see anyone else right now."

Heart attack.

"I didn't bring any cards for poker with me. What else do you have in mind?"

"Let's talk about you coming to work for me as my vet."

"So you *have* been considering the stud-farm idea."

"I'm thinking it might just work."

"Of course it will, if that's what you want to do. You know you can do anything if you're on fire for it. But it's time to give your mind and body a rest. I'll be back tomorrow morning after your surgery."

"I want you here when I wake up."

"If there's standing room."

"Stop teasing. Can I count on you?"

She could hardly breathe. Something in his tone of voice told her he didn't want to be alone. "Feral horses couldn't keep me away."

"I'm going to hold you to that. Are you going back to the trailer?"

"Where else?"

"I don't like the idea of you being there alone."

"I'm a big girl now."

"I know, but I wish you'd stay here tonight. I like the idea of Dr. Henson being here before, during and after my operation."

Beneath the banter she felt he was dead serious. She shook her head in bewilderment. *"Connor—"*

"I've gotten used to us being together. Haven't you?"

"Well, yes, but—"

"So you don't have a problem with that."

"Well, no, but—"

"Stay with me tonight."

While she felt a shiver run through her, he said, "Would you tell Wade to come in? I need to talk to him, but I want you to stay put."

The painkillers had done strange things to him. In shock over his behavior, she got up and opened the door. Wade was out in the hall talking to one of the nurses. "Connor wants to see you now."

"It took him long enough."

"He's not himself at the moment," she whispered.

Wade entered the room and moved to the side of Connor's bed. "How are you feeling?"

"Weird. Will you do me a favor and take Firebrand back to the barn at the RV park tomorrow?"

"Sure. Kim and I will exercise and feed him, too. No problem."

"Thanks. When the doctor releases me I'll take care of him until the rodeo is over."

"You won't be doing anything for at least six weeks," Liz interjected. "I'll see to the horses while you rest here in the hospital."

The nurse suddenly stepped in the room. "It's long past visiting hours."

"Uh-oh," Wade muttered. "We've been given our marching orders. Be a good cowboy and we'll see you tomorrow." Wade's blue eyes swerved to Liz. "I'll walk you out."

Making another impulsive decision because of Connor, she said, "I'm going to see if I can stay with him tonight. I'll arrange with the nurse for a cot."

The look Wade gave her sent heat rushing to Liz's face. "Then I'll say good-night to both of you."

Liz walked him to the door. "I told you he's not himself. Thank you for finding me earlier." She gave him a hug.

"You're welcome." The faint smile he gave her left her perplexed. Then he disappeared down the hall.

As she went back to sit in the chair next to Connor, the nurse came back in. Liz asked if a cot could be sent up so she could stay.

The other woman nodded. "I'll call Housekeeping."

"Thank you."

Connor's eyes filled with anxiety. "It was selfish of me to ask you to stay tonight. You need your sleep to be your best in the arena tomorrow night. You need to go."

Her heart pounded too hard. "I'm not leaving. I want to make sure you're all right. Don't worry. I'll get a good sleep on the cot."

He fastened his gaze on her. "If you're sure."

"Of course I am."

"How did you find out I got hurt?"

She moistened her lips. "On my way back from the convention center I heard my cell ring. I thought you were calling, but it turned out to be Derrick."

"He never gives up!"

"No…that wasn't why he called. He felt terrible about your accident and wanted me to know. He's one of your fans. I need to call him tomorrow and thank him for being concerned. I'm afraid that the minute he told me you'd been carted off to the hospital I had a panic attack and left him hanging."

"A real panic attack?"

"Yes. I went clammy. Wade found me at the truck and had to help me calm down so I could get ready for my event. He's a wonderful friend, Connor."

"He and I may not have survived to the last three nights, but I'm planning to give him the cut of my earnings I would have given him if we'd lasted all the way. I've made a ton of money this year. Without him, I'd be nothing."

That did bring tears. She looked down to hide them. "He'll be thrilled."

"He deserves it."

An employee from Housekeeping entered the room and put the folded cot against the wall. After he left, Liz stood and found a spot to set it up. She removed her hat and boots before stretching out on the skimpy mattress.

"This is almost like being in the trailer. I can even look down on you," Connor quipped.

Liz chuckled. "I'll admit, this is kind of fun."

His eyes never left her. "Do you mind not being able to take a shower or brush your teeth?"

She flicked him a glance. "I'll live for one night. Don't say it—"

"Say what?"

"That I'm too good to be true."

"I wasn't going to. You were sensational out there tonight."

"You saw it, even in the state you were in?"

"My friend Brian caught it on his phone camera and showed me the video after they brought me in. He just left."

"Thanks for the compliment. I told Sunflower we had to do our best for you."

"She's almost human, Liz. I'm afraid Firebrand feels deserted and could use her company."

"They'll be together tomorrow. I'll talk to him and give him a rubdown."

Connor sighed. "Will it really be six weeks before I'm normal again?"

"Afraid so. At least to begin with. But you really need to give it twelve. According to this sheet on the bedside table, you'll need to arrange for physiotherapy when you get home."

"What else?"

Liz scanned the list. "For the first three weeks you'll wear a shoulder sling and will have to avoid pendular exercises. Later you'll do gentle isometric exercises as your pain allows and be weaned off the sling. At six weeks you'll be able to drive, do light lifting and some swimming. At twelve weeks you can go riding again."

He groaned. "In twelve weeks I'll have forgotten how."

"That's okay. It's possible you'll be putting a whole new business together." *Or a whole new marriage.* "That doesn't require getting on top of a horse."

Jarod hadn't received a vision about his brother. Now she knew why, and sat there in shock.

Connor's cell phone rang, interrupting her thoughts. He frowned. "Will you see who it is?"

She reached for it. "It's your grandfather."

"Go ahead and answer it."

Liz clicked on. "Hi, Ralph. It's Liz. Your grandson is right here in the hospital bed and anxious to talk to you."

"I'm glad you're there. How is he really?"

The love in his voice was tangible. "He's in excellent shape. Connor is tough, like you." The older man laughed. "Once his tear is repaired, he'll be good as new."

"What time are they going to do it?"

"At six in the morning. He'll be able to leave the hospital by tomorrow evening or the next day. I'll be here for the whole thing," she assured him.

"Bless you." His voice cracked. "You two have made this old man proud. My cup has run over."

"So has mine. Here's Connor."

After passing him the phone, she disappeared into the bathroom to freshen up and give them some privacy before things settled down and she could rest. Hopefully more painkillers would kick in and Connor would finally sleep.

For someone who'd sustained a serious injury, he was babbling like a brook. It had to be the medication. He was hilarious, and she loved him so terribly she didn't know what to do with all her unlocked feelings running rampant.

After she'd stayed in there as long as she dared, she went back in the room, hoping he'd fallen asleep because he needed it badly. No such luck. The nurse had just finished putting something in his IV and was recording his vital signs.

"I thought you'd never come out of there." He sounded grumpy.

She couldn't prevent the chuckle that escaped. "I bet it felt good to talk to your grandfather."

"He's a fusser, but I told him I didn't want Jarod or Avery to come because I had you to look after me. You're a doctor, and you understand me, and you like me and my horse a lot. And you give us treats and entertain me better than anyone in the world."

The nurse flashed Liz a grin. "That's high praise." She mouthed the words before she left the room.

"Your praise is going to go to my head," Liz said, trying not to burst into laughter.

"They'll all fly here on the last day with your parents to watch you crowned."

"I didn't know they were giving those out. I thought it was a buckle."

"No...no." His voice was slowing down fast. "You should have been...nominated for the queen of the...rodeo."

"Queen?" He must have meant Miss Rodeo. There actually was such a person being feted in Las Vegas, but Liz couldn't understand where that thought had come from.

"You...don't...know how...beautiful...you...a..."

Even if he was delirious, she felt the impact of those words in every atom of her body. Was it the drugs talking, or were his feelings as strong as hers? She wanted to trust them, but Reva was still in the picture.

Realizing the medicine had taken effect, she pulled her boots back on and slipped outside to the nursing station. She asked that, when it came time to prep Connor for surgery, they would wake her up if she wasn't already awake.

With that request taken care of, she slipped down to the lounge to buy some chips and a cola out of the machines. Before she returned to the room, she called her parents to tell them what was going on.

The minute she heard their voices, they all shed a few tears of happiness over her results so far, but once

Connor's name was mentioned it was her father who said, "His disappointment has to be gut-wrenching."

Liz's heart was devastated for him. "Right now he's too doped up to feel much of anything. But in the days to come he's going to feel it."

"I'm glad my Lizzie girl is there for him."

Dad... "He's been so good to me, it's my chance to pay him back. I told Ralph I'd watch over him."

"I know. We've already talked to him and he was so grateful he could hardly get the words out."

"Ralph's a sweetheart."

"Honey?" her mom chimed in. "You need to get your rest. You've got three more big nights coming up."

"I know. Don't worry. Wade and his girlfriend are here for Connor, too. We'll take turns. I'd better go now, but I promise to call you tomorrow after his surgery. Love you both."

Once they'd hung up she texted Derrick to apologize for being abrupt over the phone. She wished him and his brother luck and told him she'd call him soon to talk.

A phone message had come in while she'd been with Connor. Kyle had heard the news and asked her to phone him back. But she couldn't handle an actual conversation with him right now, so she texted him with a brief report and promised to call him sometime tomorrow. Liz hurried back to Connor's room and walked over to the bed. He was out like a light. Her heart ached because the great champion had come to the end of a long journey. But a new one would be beginning.

Please, God, help him to find himself.

The hospital cot didn't do the job, but it didn't matter. She was exactly where she wanted to be, because she'd discovered that the cover of the book she'd always found the most compelling couldn't begin to compare to the substance of the man inside.

Chapter Nine

"Mr. Bannock?"

He opened his eyes. The lids felt heavy. "Are you ready for me?"

"You're back in your room. The surgery is over and you're doing fine. Your doctor will be in later."

"I can't believe it."

"Well, it's true" came the familiar female voice he longed to hear.

His eyes opened wider. "Liz—you're here!"

Her beautiful face smiled down at him. He could never get enough of the green sparkle coming from her dark-lashed eyes. "Where else would I be? I made you a promise. Don't you remember?"

"Everything's pretty hazy. Did you stay all night?"

"Of course." He noticed that the room was filled with flowers. "We've been joined at the hip for almost two weeks now. I wouldn't have deserted you."

He reached out to grasp her hand, needing her touch. "What time is it?"

"Twenty after ten in the morning."

"You should be out exercising Sunflower."

"I've got all day, but my first priority is you. On a scale of one to—"

"A two, Doctor. No more."

"That's good."

"They must have doped me up big-time."

"I spoke to the surgeon. Dr. Mason made a small incision so, in time, you probably won't see the scar. He said it was a textbook case, and you're going to be a hundred percent *if* you follow the rehab instructions to the letter.

"For your information, he's a fan of yours. In case you've reconsidered your retirement from the rodeo, he said that you're still young enough and in such good shape that in twelve weeks you could get back in training in order to win your sixth gold buckle next winter."

Connor squeezed her fingers before letting her go. "Afraid not. I meant what I told you. My rodeo days are over."

"It isn't me you need to convince. There's a world of fans out there that can't bear to think they'll never again see you fly out of the chute on Firebrand to wow everyone with your genius."

He scowled. "It's not genius, just stupidity."

Her features sobered. "You know what? We're all born into this world with a purpose and gifts. You have many gifts, and one of them has been to entertain people who can't imagine doing what you do. For a little while, it wrests them from their mundane existence to watch a champion.

"To me, it's like listening to a great concert pianist or a world-famous opera singer. How about watching a great skier win the downhill at the world championships? Or thrilling to the winner of a Formula I grand prix? You think those achievements are stupid?" Her hands formed fists. "The venue doesn't matter. It's the fact that someone has risen far beyond human expectations to make life exciting for the rest of us.

"At my autograph signing last evening, a twelve-year-old girl in a wheelchair came with her parents to get my signature. She'd been paralyzed in a car accident. Before that, she'd wanted to be a barrel racer. She told me of the pleasure it gives her to watch someone like me perform and thanked me through the tears. I've never been so humbled in my life.

"Don't you realize how exciting your career has been for Ralph, who's been doing his hardest to help his grandchildren realize their dreams? Because if you don't, then it's sad that you're so blind, Connor Bannock!" Her rebuke rang out in the room.

It reminded him of that first day in the truck, when she'd ripped him up one side and down the other. But this second chastening found its way to his inner core. While he was trying to recover, he heard voices at the door. It opened a little wider to reveal his ex-wife's silhouette. Wade and Kim stood behind her.

Those startled light blue eyes darted from Liz to him. "Conner? I got here as soon as I could. Am I interrupting something?" She sounded out of breath.

Before Connor could say anything, Liz reached for her purse. "Not at all. I was just leaving to get back to the trailer and take care of the horses. I'll call you later to see how you're doing, Connor. If you don't overdo today, the doctor said you could be released by evening." He watched her greet the others before her lovely body in her knockout shirt and jeans disappeared out the door.

Evening? *Hallelujah.*

LIZ LEFT THE hospital at a run. Anything Connor had said to her last night was the effect of the medication. *You're a lovesick fool, Liz Henson.*

Bless Wade for transporting Liz's horse to the Mack Center early. When she called him later in the day to find out Connor's condition, Wade told her the doctor said he was coming along nicely, but he shouldn't overdo it from all the phone calls and visitors. She also learned that Reva had been with him all day.

Connor had given Wade a key to get into the trailer and bring him his toiletries and a change of clothes. That meant he didn't intend to come back to the trailer. With Connor no longer able to compete and Reva there, he had incentive to leave in order to be alone with her. No doubt they would go to a hotel when he was released.

Naturally Wade wasn't about to pass on anything that Connor might have confided to him in private. It was enough to know his ex-wife had dropped everything to fly to Las Vegas. After all, she'd never stopped loving him.

Liz decided to keep her horse in the stall at the Mack Center for the duration of finals to cut down on the transporting. But, even with her usual preparations, she knew her timing was off when she raced out of the alley that evening. Lack of concentration was the culprit. Her score of 13.77 gave her a fourth place for the night. Not good. That would bring her average down.

When it was over, she removed the saddle and blanket. "It wasn't your fault," she whispered to Sunflower. "I didn't get any sleep last night and my mind couldn't focus. Worse, I did the unforgiveable and got angry with Connor right after he was out of surgery today.

I've really lost the plot, little lady, but I'll do better tomorrow."

She walked over to the other stall and walked Polly around for a little while before heading for the truck to go home. The trailer was like an empty tomb without Connor. After her shower she went straight to bed with the remote and turned on another rerun of *Keeping Up Appearances.*

In this one, Daisy had run away from her sister's house and needed to be found. Normally Liz would be laughing her head off, but not tonight. Dissolving into tears, she turned off the TV and buried her face in the pillow.

She slept late. While she fixed herself some cereal, her first thought was to phone Connor and make sure he was all right. But, if she did that, she'd be interrupting him and Reva.

If Liz could just apologize for what she'd said to him yesterday, maybe then she'd be able to get through two more nights of competition and not fall apart. For years she'd had the ability to compartmentalize her personal and professional lives. Not this time.

Wade's knock on the trailer door had her rushing to answer it. "I was just about to call you. Have you talked to Connor today? Is he all right?"

His friend eyed her steadily. "When I left his hotel room a little while ago, he looked in pretty good shape."

No mention of Reva, no mention of which hotel. Liz found it difficult to breathe. "Thank goodness."

"Yup. He asked me to check up on you." That made her heart flip-flop. "If you don't like sleeping in the trailer alone, he hopes you'll go to a hotel and has asked me to take care of you."

Pain cut her to the quick. "Both of you have enough on your minds without worrying about me. I got a good sleep last night and intend to hang out here until finals are over. Once my parents fly in with Jarod and Sadie tomorrow, we'll figure everything out to get the rig and the horses back to Montana."

"I'll tell him what you said. Do you want to go to lunch with me and Kim?"

"That's very nice, but I'm eating breakfast now and plan to stay here until it's time to drive to the center and take a little ride on Sunflower." It was nearing the end of the ten-day competition. She didn't want to wear out her horse.

He nodded. "Connor told me to tell you good luck tonight, but he knows you won't need it because you light your own fires."

She'd done that, all right, when her mouth had run away with her yesterday. He might have forgiven her once, but not a second time.

"Thanks for coming by, Wade. Thanks for everything." She hugged him before shutting the door.

THE NINTH NIGHT of the NFR finals was about to begin. Connor wanted to watch it on the hotel's big-screen TV uninterrupted. Reva had left the hotel where she'd stayed the previous night and moved to his hotel.

She was curled up on the end of the couch to watch with him. He sat up in an upholstered chair with his arm in a sling, his feet resting on an ottoman. To his relief, simple ibuprofen was doing the job for the pain. He hated taking drugs.

"I still don't understand why you wouldn't stay at the Mirage with me."

He thrust her a glance. "Because we're not married, Reva."

"But somehow living in the close quarters of the trailer with Liz Henson is different?"

They'd skirted certain issues last evening after he'd been released. But bringing up Liz's name now meant she was going for the jugular. "We pooled our resources to come to the finals together. The Hensons are our neighbors and family friends."

"She's more to you than that, so don't deny it!"

"I'm not." *I'm not.*

Those blue eyes glistened with tears. They'd always gotten to him before, but no longer. "Have you slept with her?"

His anger flared. "Have you slept with your producer friend?"

She averted her eyes. "I asked you first."

"This isn't a game, Reva. You called me and said you wanted us to get back together. But two years have gone by. Aside from the issues that broke us up before, if you can't be honest with me about him, where will that get us?"

After a silence, "We've stopped seeing each other. Yes, there was a period where I thought I cared about him and we did have an affair, but it's over."

The revelation didn't touch him. "Why?"

"After I stopped seeing him, I found out he'd been keeping a secret from me. Ginger told me he's the one responsible for getting me moved to the afternoon time slot."

Connor *knew* it had to be something like that. "In other words, they're making room for someone else on the six o'clock news."

"Yes. That's like death to me."

"I'm sorry, Reva, very sorry. I know how much you've put into your career. With your track record, you have to be aware there are other networks in other cities that would grab you up in a minute."

She got to her feet. "If I went to work at another network, the same thing would happen because I'm not getting any younger. I've thought it over and want to give it up to be a wife and mother." She eyed him hungrily. "I want to be *your* wife again and have *your* baby."

"You don't want to be a wife to a cowboy."

"But the rodeo's over for you now."

He shifted in the chair. "You just don't get it. Forget the rodeo. Ranching's my life. Every aspect of it, from the horses to the cattle. During our marriage you made it clear you hated that life."

"But a baby would—"

"Do nothing to change your feelings," he broke in. "You have to love that life the way I do. It's not for everyone, as you found out. I couldn't live in Los Angeles. It's not what I do or who I am. I'm going to be starting up a stud farm. The ranch isn't the place for you and your special talents in front of the camera." He could hear Liz's voice. "You have a unique gift not given to everyone and need to use it, Reva. We were young and thought we could make it work. It pains me that we couldn't."

"So you're saying it's impossible for us?"

They stared at each other. "Isn't it? Be honest."

"How about *you* being honest. I asked you once. Now I'm going to ask you again. Have you taken Liz Henson to bed yet?"

He took a deep breath. "No."

That seemed to shake her. "So she's not the reason you don't want to get back together?"

"Stop trying to find a reason when we both know what it is. Our attorney defined it. *Incompatibility* in the truest sense of the word. But I'll give you another reason I couldn't have given you two years ago, because at that point I was too devastated to think."

"What is it?" she murmured.

"I'm no longer in love with you."

Reva backed away from him. "I know." Her voice shook. "I can tell."

"If you'll be honest with yourself, you'll admit you're no longer in love with me, either, only the idea of it. That's what broken dreams are all about. But I'll treasure the memories of those early days when anything seemed possible. Time can't take that away from us."

Angry color filled her cheeks. She reached for her purse and started walking toward the door. Connor got up from the chair and followed her. She turned to him. "There's a big difference between you and me. I'm afraid I'll never get over you. Goodbye, Connor." She kissed his cheek before walking out into the hall.

He watched for a minute and then closed the door. All he felt was a liberating sense of relief that, at last, this period of his life was over. And maybe he felt a little guilt, because his mind was already somewhere else. After going back to his chair, he increased the volume on the remote. The rodeo was halfway over. He'd missed the steer wrestling. Three more events until it was time for the barrel racing.

Connor reached for the coffee he'd been drinking

and finished it off while he watched each performance. Team roping was up next. Derrick was the heeler in the Porter brothers' duo. His aim was off tonight and he only roped one hind leg of the steer, costing them a five-second penalty. That was too bad.

As the time grew closer to Liz's event, his stomach muscles tightened into knots. They'd never cramped up on him this badly prior to one of his own events. Good old Wade was there, watching over her, and would keep in touch with Connor. While he sat there held in the grip of gut-wrenching nerves, his cell phone rang.

He glimpsed Jarod's name on the caller ID and clicked on. "If it had been anyone else phoning right now…"

"I hear you. How are you holding up, bro?"

"Ask me after Liz's event is over. Is everyone with you?"

"We're all glued to the TV, too."

"She had to be upset about last night's score. That was my fault for asking her to stay overnight with me at the hospital the night before."

"You mean—"

"When I told her I didn't want her to leave, she arranged for a cot," Connor cut in. "That was selfish of me. She couldn't have gotten a decent sleep on that thing."

"I have news for you. No one slept well last night."

Connor let out a heavy sigh. "If you've got any special Crow prayers for her…"

"Liz doesn't need them."

"You sound like your uncle when he's looking off into a place no one else can see."

"All you have to do is visualize her doing what she

does best and you'll have no worries. Take care of yourself."

"I am. Wade and Kim have been waiting on me when Liz couldn't."

"That's good to know. We'll see you tomorrow."

"Tell Grandpa I love him." Emotion overtook him and he started to choke up. "Tell him I'm grateful for everything he's ever done for me."

Jarod's voice sounded oddly husky when he said, "He already knows, but you can tell him yourself after we get you home."

After *we* get you home?

No way. There was only one person who was going to get him home. *Sorry, Kyle.*

He clicked off to watch the last of the bareback riding, but his nerves were making him fidgety. He rubbed his scruffy jaw while he waited for the barrel racing to start.

One of the workers rode out on the rake to groom the arena. Besides maintaining a consistent, level footing, the machine repaired and regraded the footing layer. Connor wanted everything perfect for Liz.

The sounds of the crowd swelled as the first twelve racers clocked their times. Liz was thirteenth out. He held his breath when her name was announced. Unable to sit still, he got to his feet and moved closer to the TV. Suddenly, she hurtled out of the alley. She swished around those barrels like she was playing a seamless game of Quidditch at Hogwarts from a Harry Potter film. No extra movements.

Sunflower was an extension of her. Elegance personified, that was Liz. His heart warmed in his chest to watch her gallop home. A huge roar went up from the crowd over her sensational score of 13.40, but no sound was as loud as his own cry of joy. She'd set the bar high for tonight's competition.

Dustine Hoffman was the last one out. She was a tough one to beat by anyone's standards. Her style reminded him of a pianist who moved her whole body back and forth while she played at the keyboard. Lots of elbow and footwork. Her long hair flew behind her like a pennant. She clocked a 13.44.

You did it, Liz.

He couldn't stay alone in this hotel room another second. Without hesitation he called the front desk and told them he was checking out. He asked them to send someone to carry his overnight case and to call him a taxi.

On the way to the RV park, he asked the driver to stop at the all-night supermarket where he'd shopped with Liz before. He found some fresh-cut daisies in a vase and paid for them, along with a bag of Snickers bars. In another ten minutes he let himself inside the trailer. The driver brought in his case for him. Liz had left a light on.

It felt so good to be home again, he didn't care about being sling tied for the rest of the month. The faint scent of her fragrance hung in the air. When Liz got back later, another buckle would be added to their centerpiece.

She'd left it in the middle of the table. He put the vase of flowers next to it, along with two candy bars. The rest he set on the counter. After he took another dose of antibiotic, he fixed himself a cheese-and-bologna sandwich with one hand. It was tricky, because he was right-handed, but he managed. Then he settled down on the couch to watch TV and eat.

Wade phoned. He was higher than a kite over her win. Connor told him Reva was gone forever. The revelation was met with silence. Connor took it to mean Wade was glad for him but didn't dare say anything.

Connor helped him out by telling him he'd moved back to the trailer, but asked him not to tell Liz. He wanted to surprise her. They chatted for a moment about the steer wrestling. Wade informed him of Jocko's win. "That's good."

"With you out of the finals, he stands a good chance of winning the whole thing. I admit he has a lot of try," Wade commented before they hung up. Yup. Jocko would no doubt win his first world championship.

Since Liz had to go to the eleven o'clock buckle ceremony at the South Point before coming home, it would be a while before she walked through the door.

It was a Friday night, so her favorite reruns ought to be on. He found the channel featuring the British comedies and discovered the show about Hyacinth would be on in five more minutes. He was curious to find out what Liz thought was so hilarious and decided to record it so they could watch it together after she returned.

The news bored him. With time hanging heavy, he found his electric razor and went into the bathroom to do something about his beard. After two days it was driving him crazy. He was almost through when he saw Liz coming toward him looking shell-shocked. She tossed her hat and purse on a chair.

"Connor—I didn't know. I—I didn't realize you were here," she stammered.

"Yup. I'm back." He finished the under part of his chin before shutting the razor off.

"But I thought you'd be staying at a hotel from now on."

"So you didn't miss me and wish I'd stayed away?"

Her brows formed a distinct frown. "I didn't say that. Don't put words in my mouth. I'm just surprised, that's all."

"The only reason I got myself a hotel room was to give everyone a break. I could just call room service when I needed something."

Liz looked away from him. Maybe he was mistaken, but he thought her face had lost a little color. "You should be in bed."

"I'll get there, Doctor, but since I need to sleep downstairs, do you mind spending the rest of the time in the niche?"

"No," she blurted. "I'll change the sheets on both beds right now."

"While you do that, I'll fix you a peanut-butter sandwich and a glass of milk. You need food after your outstanding win tonight."

Her chin lifted. "You saw it?"

He nodded. "Before I left the hotel. The arena hasn't seen a score like 13.40 in years. You're on the verge of walking away with the whole thing. My heart was in my throat when you and Sunflower flew back to the alley."

A fetching smile appeared at one corner of her mouth. He'd been waiting for some sign that she was glad to see him. "So was mine. I'm afraid there'll be no encore tomorrow night."

"Don't worry. All you'll need to do is your best. It'll be enough."

"Since when did you start seeing the glass as full?"

"Rooming with you has something to do with it. After you make the beds, we'll celebrate your victory. Where's your buckle?"

"In my purse."

"Be sure to add it to our centerpiece." Before she got out the clean linen, she took the box from her purse and put it on top of the others.

"Daisies!" Her eyes shone. "They're beautiful. Thank you, Connor."

"I wish they were roses, but no florists were open tonight. That makes four for you."

He fixed her a sandwich, but he couldn't keep his eyes off her feminine lines and curves while she used the ladder to get her work done. Once the beds were made, they ate and watched TV.

"I have one more surprise for you."

"You've done too much already."

"I did it for me, too." He turned on the program.

"You recorded *Keeping Up Appearances!*" The pleasure in her voice made it all worth it.

"I want to see what's so funny."

"She's a scream, Connor."

Halfway through the program, he could see what she meant. Hyacinth was being chased through a field by a bull. The faces she pulled and the contortions she went through in order to extricate herself had him laughing out loud. "They should pay her to come to the arena and put on this act. It would bring the house down."

Their gazes met. "It really would. You've made this a perfect night, but you look tired. Let me help you get ready for bed." She shot out of the chair to find him clean pajamas. In the end, he kept on the Western shirt he'd been wearing and put on the bottoms. While he was in the bathroom, she'd changed into her own nightwear. She put his medicine and water by the head of the couch. With teeth brushed and lights out, they got into their beds. He had to lie flat on his back to accommodate his sling.

This time, she was the one who looked down on him. Those fabulous green eyes and her smile healed every wound. He knew he would have to see her every day and night and all the seconds in between for the rest of his life, or it wasn't worth living.

"The doctor is in. If you need me in the night, just call out."

Lady, you have no idea what you've just said.

Chapter Ten

Liz's cell phone rang at 8:00 a.m. She clicked on. "Hi, Mom. I was about to call you." She'd just fixed breakfast for Connor and had helped him off with his shirt. His cut physique was something to behold. She trembled just thinking about him. Now he was in the bathroom getting ready for the day, but he'd need her help putting on a clean shirt when he came out.

"We're on our way to the airport. Zane's driving us in his car."

"I can't wait to see all of you."

"We feel the same. Our flight from Billings leaves in two hours. Connor's family will meet us there."

"Who's tending Ryan?"

"Jarod and Sadie drove him out to the reservation to stay with his uncle's family. They're crazy about him."

"I miss him. I miss all of you. Who's going to be with Ralph?"

"Besides the household staff, his brother Tyson."

"That's good. I'll give him a call before my event."

"He'll love that. It won't be long now, honey. We're scheduled to arrive in Las Vegas at two. Sadie called last week and said she and Jarod had made reservations at the Venetian for all of us. It was very thoughtful of her. You'll need to let your friend Kyle know where we're staying."

Liz took an unsteady breath. "Our plans have changed. He's not coming. I'll tell you why later."

"Oh, honey..." She heard her mother's dejection.

"It's for the best, Mom. Really, it is. Give me a ring when you've reached the hotel. I'm going to work with Sunflower early so I can spend time with you before we all have to head for the arena."

"I guess I don't need to tell you how proud we are of you. I didn't know I could cry so many happy tears. Your father's going around in a daze."

"I'm in a daze, too. Get here safely."

"We will. Love you."

Connor came out of the bathroom as she was cleaning up the kitchen. He had a dark green-and-black-plaid shirt in his hand. "Do you mind helping me into this?"

Oh, Connor. If you only knew.

Smothering a groan from the unassuaged ache she felt for him, she eased him into it with great care and buttoned him up. He was a heartbreaker, all right, from the sun-bleached tips of his wavy hair to his well-worn Justin cowboy boots, one of his other sponsors.

"You smell good," she commented.

His eyes bored into hers. "We wear the same perfume," he teased. "By the way, that long-sleeved navy shirt looks terrific on you."

"Thanks." She forced herself to step away from him. "Everyone will be at the Venetian after two."

"It'll be a great reunion. Wade and Kim will pick me up there. We have front-row seats at the arena right by our families."

A deep pain passed through her. "Connor—when

we started out, we had no idea what was going to happen to you. It kills me that you're not going to be performing in that arena tonight."

He studied her for a minute out of those intelligent brown eyes. "Do you want to know the truth? I'm glad things worked out exactly as they have. For the first time in my rodeo career, I'm going to be sitting in the arena with the people I love, watching someone I admire more than you could possibly imagine. That person is you."

She picked up a throb in his voice she couldn't ignore.

"Tonight, Liz Henson, you're going to win the world championship. I wouldn't miss this experience for anything on earth. It's been my honor and privilege getting to know the you who has been hidden from me."

She stood there without moving.

Did he just say, "It's been my honor and privilege?"

Had those words been meant as the most beautiful goodbye speech she'd ever heard? Had he and Reva decided to get remarried and make it work this time? If a person could die of heartache, she was a prime candidate.

He brushed his mouth against her cheek before he reached for his cowboy hat. "I'll wait in the truck for you. Mind driving me to the hotel on the way? I want Wade and Kim to have a day off from worrying about me, so I'm going to stay in Jarod and Sadie's room until our families arrive."

Despite her shaking body, Liz managed to get ready, then drive him to the hotel. She was glad he was going to rest in his brother's hotel room where he could enjoy room service. Her heart aching for him, she dropped him off and drove to the center to check on Sunflower. On this last day of competition, she walked her around on foot for a little while, with no expectations, in order to give her a rest.

"Tonight will be the last time, little lady," she whispered.

As for Polly, she needed some exercise, so Liz rode her around. This horse would be happy to get home where they could take some trail rides. She didn't like been cooped up. For that matter, neither did Sunflower, who had to be tired of ten days' competition.

After grabbing a quick bite to eat at a drive-through, Liz went to the hotel and discovered the families had just arrived. The reunion with loved ones was an emotional one. She had to fight tears. Around five o'clock they all left the hotel for the Mack Center.

She watched in despair over Connor, who was unable to compete. It wasn't fair. He drove away with Wade and Kim, his arm in a sling. The others left in a taxi, while she drove over to the arena with her father.

After she parked the truck, she leaned across and hugged him. "I love you, Dad. I would never have made it this far without you."

"Sure, you would have, but I'm glad you didn't have to. You've given me thrill after thrill so far in this life. And there'll be a lot more of that coming after the rodeo is behind you."

She knew what he was trying to tell her, but when you were in pain…

It was time to go inside.

"You really like the knotted reins?"

"Definitely."

"Connor knew what he was talking about."

"Yes."

"He seems to be in a lot better emotional shape than I would have expected."

She agreed, which was no surprise since he and Reva had probably reconciled for good. "Connor's tough, like Ralph and Jarod."

"Ralph calls you two his champions."

She smiled. "I know. I talked to him and Tyson on the phone for a few minutes, back at the hotel."

He grasped the hand closest to him. "Go out there tonight and have the time of your life."

She nodded, but it would be hard to do, knowing Connor was just a spectator this time.

"Whatever happens will happen, Lizzie girl. Just remember how wonderful the journey has been."

Especially the journey with Connor. A time out of time, never to be repeated.

As usual, her father gave the best advice. "I'll remember."

"We'll meet you out here after it's over."

They parted company and she headed inside to mount up one more time. The earthy scent of horses and cattle drifted throughout, making the National Finals Rodeo a full sensory experience she'd never forget.

Liz walked past the same contestants getting ready for their events. It was concentration time. She rounded the row of stalls, then gasped. Sunflower was lying against the side of her stall in a horrible position.

The first rule in a crisis was to avoid frightening her horse. At a glance, she could see Sunflower was stall cast. She'd gotten so tired she'd lain down, rolled against the wall and was trapped. Without enough room for leverage to stand up, she'd injured her legs.

"It's all right." Liz hunkered down and spoke to her, patting her neck. "I'm going to find help for you. Don't panic, little lady. I'll be right back."

She crept out of the stall and found the two assigned livestock helpers, who rushed forward. Between the three of them, they got Sunflower on her feet. During the whole procedure she spoke gently to her favorite horse, who was struggling with fright. If she panicked, she could go into shock.

"You're all right now," Liz said, over and over again. Carefully she ran her hands over Sunflower's legs. There was no bleeding, so she hadn't been in that position long, thank heaven. But those tendons would be sore.

Tears ran down Liz's cheeks as she flung her arms around her mare's neck. "You've given it your all, Sunflower. You're the best. No one ever had a better horse. Tomorrow I'm taking you home."

Joe, one of the older helpers she'd gotten to know, tapped her on the shoulder. "Your event's up next."

"I know. I'm going to have to ride Polly."

"Don't you worry about this horse. I'll stay here and gentle her until you come back."

She sniffed. "I'm indebted to you, Joe. Keep her warm with this light blanket." Liz threw it over her horse and gave her a treat.

"Everything's going to be all right, Liz. You go out there on your other horse and you'll do fine."

Fine wasn't good enough. *Jarod's vision hadn't foreseen this catastrophe.*

With a nod, she carried her gear and saddle to the next stall. "Polly? It's you and me in the spotlight now." She got the horse ready and walked her out.

Joe smiled at her as she passed. "Your horse is settling down."

"You have no idea how much I appreciate your help."

"That's what I'm here for."

"See you soon, Sunflower."

Once mounted, she headed for the area where the other barrel racers were assembled. The first one took off. She heard the roar of the crowd.

Liz could visualize Connor and her loved ones out there waiting to see her performance. Her heart plummeted to her feet.

Get hold of yourself, Liz. You need to put that picture away and visualize what you have to do for this go-round.

"Our turn's coming up, Polly. All we can do is our best. The first barrel is a blind barrel compared to the outside runs. We're going to take Dad's advice. We're going to run out that alley and you're going to hunt for that barrel as if your life depended on it."

She patted her neck. "You're going to hunt it and kill that turn. You've done it before in practice—you can do it again. Do it for Connor. He's done everything to help me win. Now we need your help, Polly."

IN THE STANDS, Connor looked down the row of familiar faces. Both families were spread out on the seats, with Wade and his girlfriend next to Connor. Jarod and Sadie sat on his other side by Millie and Mac. Zane and Avery sat next to them.

Where was Kyle, Liz's supposed favorite? How come he hadn't shown up yet? Maybe he was sitting somewhere else, but that seemed odd to Connor with her parents here.

Though they'd all enjoyed the other events and cheered Jocko, who'd taken over Connor's place as world champion this year, their group grew quiet, knowing the barrel racing was about to begin.

This was it, the moment Liz had been training for since she was a young girl. It was amazing her mentor father could function right now.

The noise of the crowd reached a crescendo as the first barrel racer entered the arena. Connor watched her and the subsequent four riders who appeared in quick succession. They clocked good times of 13.80, 13.77, 13.74. The other knocked over barrels for a five-second penalty. One by one, more barrel racers put up their times. 13.72, two 13.70s. The scores were stacking up.

"Dustine Hoffman, riding Cranky tonight, is next to last in the lineup. She's number one in earnings coming into the finals this year. We'll see if last year's world champion can do it again."

Connor gritted his teeth, knowing this was the rider Liz had to beat. He watched her shoot out of the alley, but he could tell she was being more careful than usual so she wouldn't knock over a barrel. Whoops. She took the third one a little too wide and finished with a 13.78. Not a winning time this go-round. His body sagged in relief.

Then came the announcement he'd been waiting for. It zapped through him like a bolt of lightning. "The winner in three rounds here at finals, with the best score on her first round, and second in earnings is up next. Liz Henson from Montana on Sunflower! Hold on. I've just been told there's been a change of horses. She's riding Polly."

Polly?

Connor broke out in a cold sweat.

"No—" Sadie cried in anguish.

He and Jarod shared a pained glance. Wade leaned closer. "Something has happened to Sunflower."

Yup. Polly, a reddish-brown bay with a black mane and tail, had never competed here, though Liz had trained her well. This arena was small and a horse had to be aggressive to careen around the barrels. She didn't have Sunflower's speed.

Connor got a sick feeling in the pit of his stomach. Instead of sitting with everyone, he should have gone back to the stall to be with Liz before the events started. But he'd been afraid he might distract her. With his arm useless right now, he'd never felt so helpless in his life.

If Liz was going to have a shot at this last round, it was because Polly wasn't exhausted after competing nine rounds in nine days.

Suddenly she galloped out of the alley. Connor was on his feet as she circled the first barrel. Polly shot across to the second barrel with unbelievable energy, circling it so closely, he couldn't believe she didn't touch it.

One more barrel to go, Liz. He started to feel light-headed with excitement and sat down again. Then the thing happened that signaled the death knell. She bumped against the third barrel.

Pain tore his guts apart. Unable to look, he closed his eyes in excruciating pain before hearing the ear-splitting roar of the crowd.

"You can open them now, bro. The barrel didn't tip over."

What?

Jarod wore one of his rare brilliant smiles.

It had to be a miracle! Most of the time in practice the barrels didn't fall, but during the competition you could count on them going down.

When Connor looked over at the score he saw a 13.67. His mouth went so dry he couldn't swallow, let alone talk. Before he knew it, the event had come to an end and her score stood.

Jarod turned to him. "She won, bro. She's won the whole shootin' match. I'd hug you, but we don't want to do any damage to that incision."

The others were on their feet, jumping up and down for joy. Wade said, "Kim and I are going to find her."

"Tell her I'll be right there."

Sadie and Millie were embracing while he made his way over to Mac and shook his hand. "I hope you know she won this championship for her champion father."

He wiped his eyes. "I was no champion, but Millie and I gave birth to one. Thank you for getting her here safe and sound. I believe it made all the difference. We're so sorry about your accident."

"I'd forgotten all about it." It was the truth.

Avery hugged him on his good side. "Mac was right. Bringing Liz with you gave her the kind of confidence to put her over the top. You were always my hero, but you've outdone yourself this time."

After she kissed his cheek, Zane shook his hand. "I've never been to a rodeo until tonight. To think you won five times in this arena is phenomenal."

"I got lucky."

He grinned. "Sure you did. I guess Liz just got lucky, too."

Millie turned to him and gave him a gentle hug. "Bless you for taking such wonderful care of our daughter despite the terrible disappointment to yourself."

His throat swelled. "I would have liked to be doing this for her a long time ago, but Daniel Corkin got in the way." At that remark, her eyes flared in surprise. "Shall we go find her in the back before we drive over to the South Point?"

On their way out of the arena it occurred to him that Kyle might have been here the whole time helping Liz. It wasn't a pleasant thought.

Wade intercepted him when they reached the stall area. "Sunflower got stall cast, but she'll be fine." Connor grimaced. He figured it might have been something like that. "My rig's out in back. Why don't I load Sunflower and Polly and drive them to the RV park for the night while you go on to the South Point with your family."

"I owe you more than you'll never know, Wade."

His blue eyes smiled. "It works both ways, and you know it."

Connor followed him but held back while he watched the crowd around Liz give her hugs and congratulations. He didn't see another man around. What had happened to Kyle?

While Wade was leading her horses out of their stalls, she swung around to say something, but stopped when she saw Connor. Though her face shone with happiness, he glimpsed a shadow of sorrow in her eyes. Because Kyle wasn't here?

He moved closer. "Well…shall we add up the earnings for the world-champion barrel racer? You've won over two hundred thousand dollars."

"That last barrel should have toppled," she said in a shaky voice.

"But it didn't. Now you've got enough money to finish paying off your loans, buy yourself a new truck and car and still have money left over."

A stillness enveloped them. "It was never about the money."

"Like I told you a long time ago, you're too good to be true."

Her features hardened. "Yup. That's me."

"Where's your favorite? The one who was flying down from Bozeman?"

If he wasn't mistaken, those green eyes glittered. "At the last minute there was an emergency and he couldn't make it. But we'll see each other after I get back home. He's going to help me pick out a new truck."

The hell he was.

"Then why don't we pile everyone in my truck and head on over to the casino where you'll be royally feted. It'll be a tight squeeze, but I'm pretty sure no one will mind. I'll ask Jarod to drive us."

LIZ COULDN'T BELIEVE it when Connor managed the seating arrangements so the two of them were in back with her parents. Since it was a bit of a squeeze, he told her it might be better if she sat on his left leg so his sore arm had more room. Jarod drove with Sadie and Zane up front.

It was like déjà vu, reminding her of the night at the swimming pool when he'd pulled her onto his lap. Only, at that particular time, they'd been alone, and for a few minutes he'd kissed her with such hunger she'd started devouring him back, unable to help herself.

The memory of those moments of abandon sent a wave of heat through her sensitized body. She needed to get off him, but Saturday night in Las Vegas at the culmination of the rodeo had made the traffic impossible. Crowds of people arriving at the hotel slowed their progress. Jarod dropped them off before going to find a parking place.

To neutralize her body's reaction to their nearness, she phoned Ralph, who sounded completely overjoyed by her win. She shed tears for the love in his voice before they hung up. When she got out of the truck, she still reeled from the sensation of feeling Connor's strong heartbeat against her back. Liz throbbed to her fingertips. That was the last time she would ever get physically close to him. Reva had first rights.

As soon as she flew back to the ranch with her family, she'd let Jarod know she planned to take the vet job on the reservation and rent a house there. It wouldn't take her long to make the daily drive to the clinic in White Lodge. She'd make both jobs work if it killed her!

For the next hour she sat with the other world-championship winners behind the master of ceremonies. Her loved ones watched from one of the tables in the audience, but the only person she could see was Connor, dressed in jeans and his black shirt, and of course his white sling.

Exciting as the awards ceremony turned out to be, it hurt that Jocko Mendez was getting the gold buckle meant for Connor. She couldn't erase the tragedy from her mind, not even when it was her turn to say a few words before receiving the fabulous gold buckle she would always treasure.

"I'm reminded of a quote by Victor Hugo, one of my favorite authors. He said, 'There is nothing like a dream to create the future.' I'm here tonight living my future due to my two wonderful parents, Millie and Mac Henson, sitting out in this audience. They sacrificed everything for me and my dream. Will you please stand?"

She knew her modest parents wouldn't like this part. "Mom and Dad, this buckle's for you. My dad was a fabulous bull rider in his twenties and taught me everything I know, including about being on the back of a horse."

When they got to their feet, the crowd clapped and cheered. After the noise quieted down, they regained their seats.

"There are many people to thank. First, my best friend Sadie Bannock, a horse lover who always believed in me. I also want to acknowledge my next-door neighbor from Montana who's been my absolute inspiration for years. Neither he nor his grandfather, Ralph, another rodeo champion, would let me give up when I blew it at my first junior rodeo competition years ago. He's my idea of the all-American cowboy, and he, along with his hazer, Wade Torney, got me and my horses safely here for this great rodeo. Connor Bannock, will you please stand?"

At the mention of his name, the place literally exploded. Everyone was on their feet chanting, "Connor, Connor," before they gave him a thunderous ovation. Slowly he stood as the clapping went on and on.

"To this five-time world-champion bulldogger goes my heartfelt thanks."

The second the awards were over, Liz slipped down

to the table with her box and hugged everyone except Connor. He eyed her strangely. "*I've* been your inspiration?"

"Don't be absurd, Connor. Of course you have!"

"Now she tells me."

"Come on, everyone," Jarod spoke up. "Let's all head over to our hotel so we can party."

Liz's heart shriveled. It was the midnight hour. With her dream fulfilled, she now had to figure out her new life.

"Connor?" He stood a little distance off looking undeniably handsome. She walked over to him. "I don't know what your plans are, but if it's all right with you, I'll go by the trailer in the morning and pack up my things. Wade said he and your handlers would trailer our horses home in their rigs."

To her shock, he shook his head. "I'm taking Firebrand and Sunflower home in my trailer."

"You mean Reva's going to drive?" She thought she might die on the spot from pain.

"No."

"I don't understand."

"Reva is out of the picture and has gone back to L.A. for good."

Liz started to feel faint. "You're not making sense. You were with her yesterday."

He nodded. "After I left the hospital, I had a talk in private with her. She'd already checked in to another hotel, but we met in mine."

She rubbed her palms against her hips nervously. "I see."

"I doubt it. Reva wanted us to get back together again, but I told her that wasn't possible because I wasn't in love with her anymore. I haven't been for a long time."

The blood pounded in Liz's ears. She didn't know what to say and swallowed hard.

"But how can you take the horses back when you're not supposed to drive?"

"I'll get one of the guys to help me."

"But if you fly, you won't have so much discomfort to your arm and shoulder."

"I despise flying unless I have to."

What? "I didn't know that."

"There are a lot of things you don't know about me, but Wade's waiting to drive me to the Venetian. I'll meet you there. We can talk about this later. My only concern is for you, though it's obvious you've got family to take care of you. But you should know by now I wanted to be the one to do the honors."

Liz was dying inside. "You already did enough by driving me here."

"Not nearly enough," he muttered, "but that's a conversation for another time."

To HER ASTONISHMENT, he sought out his friends and they left the ballroom. Sadie and Jarod walked over to her. "Are you all right? You look dazed. What did Connor say to you?"

Liz stared at her friend. Tonight at the awards ceremony she'd talked about a dream that created the future, but Connor's dream had taken several unexpected turns. She was afraid he was already sinking into a depression.

"I don't know what to do. He insists on one of the

guys driving him back to the ranch with the horses, but that wouldn't be good for him."

Sadie blinked. "What about Reva?"

"That's what I asked him. He said it's over. She's gone back to Los Angeles for good."

"For *now,* you mean, until she comes after him again. That's been their pattern, and he continues to let it happen because he can't seem to help himself." Sadie looked at Jarod, who didn't say anything.

As far as Liz was concerned, they'd both just verified her tortured thoughts. Despite the fact that he'd kissed Liz with passion, she couldn't forget the way he'd looked at Reva when he'd seen her in the trailer. Liz hadn't been able to handle it and had ducked into the bathroom.

"Jarod? Is it true your brother doesn't like to fly?"

Once in a while he wore an inscrutable expression. "Is that what he told you?"

"He said he despised it."

Sadie grasped his arm. "Then *you* can drive him, darling. I'll fly back with Liz and the others tomorrow."

Jarod looked down at his wife and gave her a kiss. "Since Connor didn't ask me, I think we have to leave it up to him what he wants to do. Come on, mother of Little Sits in the Center."

Sadie stared at him with a smile. "Little Sits in the Center?"

"That's Connor's name for our baby. Didn't you know? Let's go. Everyone's waiting for us out at the truck."

But on the way back to the Venetian with her family, Liz couldn't shake off the feeling that Connor was in bad emotional shape. As soon as they'd all congregated in Jarod's suite, she walked over to his brother, who was standing next to Avery.

She hugged Liz. "I've never been so proud of anyone, ever!"

"Thanks, Avery. That means the world coming from you."

When Zane called to her, Liz was left alone with Connor for a minute.

"Connor? I've given this some thought. You shouldn't plan to drive home with one of the guys. Then you'll have to act all tough."

"I'll be all right."

Liz took a deep breath, deciding to plunge in. "You'll be a lot better if you let *me* drive us back. I'm the doctor, remember? Don't forget, I have a supply of your favorite medicine on hand—chocolate. We'll take it slow and easy to give you and the horses plenty of rest. You won't have to pretend anything with me. After all you've done for me, it's my turn to look after your needs."

The second his brown eyes ignited, she knew she'd said the right thing. "Have you asked one of the guys yet?"

"No. And, frankly, I can't wait to start back. I liked it better when it was just the two of us."

"I did, too." *It was heaven on earth.*

Chapter Eleven

"Thanks, Wade! See you back home. We'll settle up there."

Connor waved off his friend, who'd hitched up Connor's truck to the trailer and loaded the horses. Now it was time to head back to Montana with Liz at the wheel and no one else around....

If he thought he'd been nervous before he'd approached her at the arena prior to this trip to Vegas, that was nothing compared to his anxiety now. He'd allowed her to believe he was afraid to fly in order to gain her sympathy. It was a lie, although he actually did despise all the stuff you had to go through. Still, it didn't hurt if she was worried he had a bit of a phobia and had offered to drive him. He needed to be alone with her.

Liz started the truck. After Wade pulled away in his own rig, she followed them onto the road that would lead out of the RV park to the main street. This morning she was wearing his favorite red-and-blue-plaid hombre shirt. Now that he wasn't driving, he could stare at her profile and shape whenever he felt like it, which was all the time.

"How was Sunflower when you loaded her? Do you think she's still suffering?"

"She seems in pretty good shape. Our horses were nickering when Wade and I put them in the trailer."

Connor smiled. "I noticed. She was probably confiding her problems to Firebrand. You can tell they're glad to be together."

"I wouldn't doubt it. Fortunately she wasn't stall cast very long. We'll make the same number of stops on the way home so they won't get too tired." She eyed him. "Before we leave Las Vegas, do you have enough antibiotic to get home on, or should we stop and get more?"

"My other doc ordered me a two-week prescription."

He heard her chuckle over his little joke. "That's good. You need to take all of it."

"Yes, Dr. Henson."

"Any time you get tired of sitting in the same position, I'll pull over so you can get out and stretch your legs."

"I'll take my break with our children. Thanks for coming back to the trailer with me last night. I'm sure our families understood I wanted to get an early start this morning."

"To be honest, I did, too. There's nothing like a party when it's over."

"But it was a great party while it lasted, right? You're the world champion."

She darted him a searching glance. "So are you. Until your accident, it was the most wonderful experience of my life."

"Accidents happen, Liz."

He heard her deep sigh. "Did you ever see that old film, *An Affair to Remember?*"

"I did. That was one of my grandmother's favorites. While she cried over the last scene, Jarod and I made faces at each other. We were too young at the time to appreciate it. Years later I saw it again."

"Then you'll understand what was in my heart when I saw you lying on that hospital bed after you came out of surgery. As the vulnerable hero said to the crippled heroine, 'If anyone had to have an accident, why did it have to be you?' That was exactly how I felt."

His pulse sped up. "If the producers had made a sequel, we would have seen him helping her get back on her feet while she supported him in his fledgling career. That's the power of true love. So, tell me, what are you going to do with your buckle? Wear it or display it?"

"When I move out, I'll give it to my folks and let them decide."

His brows met in a frown. "What do you mean, move out?"

"I've decided I'm going to take that job on the reservation and rent a house there. Once I've talked it over with Dr. Rafferty, I'm sure I can make both jobs work."

He ground his teeth. "Does this mean my job offer is out?"

"Connor—you weren't really serious."

"Now you've wounded me again. I think this is the third time."

"If I have, please forgive me."

"I might, with one provision."

"What's that?"

"That you reconsider and come to work for me. You're the person who reminded me of an old dream and gave it a new twist. Something else you're going to learn about me is that I'm deadly serious when I decide to go after something I want."

Funny how she suddenly had to correct the steering.

Taking advantage of the palpable silence, he said, "Have you decided what kind of a truck you're going to buy?"

"After winning at the Dodge Ram finals, I guess I'd better get one of their models."

"That might be a good idea, considering you're their reigning barrel champion. Think how the words *Bannock Feral Stud Farm* will look on a big black one, unless Kyle thinks you should pick out a white one. Personally, I think black makes a statement. I'll have the same words put on this truck."

He watched her hands grip the steering wheel tighter. "Assuming you're not putting me on, how much would you pay me?"

"To work for me, one hundred thousand dollars to start, but it will be negotiable when the business starts to grow. I'll pay for your insurance, too. Maybe you and Doc Rafferty can work something out for part time at the clinic, but the job on the reservation wouldn't be possible. Jarod will have to understand.

"You can write off your new truck as a business expense. As soon as we get back to the ranch, I'll be sitting down with my attorney."

"You're serious...." She sounded shaken.

"I don't know what more to say to convince you. The ranch has plenty of land to erect an office, new barns with paddocks, breeding stalls, feed, everything I'll require. The only thing I don't have nailed down yet is the perfect vet. That's you. I bet you already know more about ferals than most vets out of med school. What we don't know we can learn together."

"Connor—"

"Hold on," he interrupted her. "All I ask is that you think about it while I sleep for a little while. The second you get tired, pull off the road. We're in no hurry."

He could tell she was getting ready to erupt in that endearing way of hers. "Is this the real reason you wanted to be alone with me?"

"It's *one* of my real reasons. I need time to explain everything, and that's what we've got while we're on the road. Time and the kind of privacy I require to talk it all out."

"So you're not really afraid of flying?"

"No. I hardly ever lie, but in this case it was an emergency. Do you hate me?"

She let out a sound of exasperation. "You could have talked to me about it after we flew home."

"But I was worried it might be too late and you wouldn't listen to me, not if you're excited to see Kyle. He might have other plans for you that could influence you one way or the other. How serious is it between the two of you?"

"Is this part of the job interview?"

"Yes. I need to know the truth. Are you going to get married on me just when I'm getting my business started, and then tell me you're moving to Bozeman?"

Silence reigned in the cab. "We're not that close. Though I like him a lot, I've decided I won't be seeing him anymore."

"But you let me believe that, about him helping you pick out a truck."

She sucked in her breath. "I guess I did."

"Can I assume you told him not to come to Las Vegas?"

"Yes, if you must know."

"Thank you for being honest with me. Now that you've laid one of my fears to rest, what else would stand in the way of your accepting my offer?"

He could hear her mind working. "Let me think about it. Tonight we'll be in Kemmerer. Before we go to bed, I'll give you an answer one way or the other."

"Promise?"

She darted him a frosty glance. "This time I'm not lying. Normally...I don't," she added.

"Anyone is capable of it, depending on the depth of their desperation."

"Are you telling me you were so desperate to get me alone, you resorted to a lie?"

"I told you. I was afraid." He laid his head back and closed his eyes. "Wake me up if you need me."

Liz found herself glancing at him many times before they reached Kemmerer. He'd called ahead to reserve a place at the same RV park for them to spend the night. The lines around his eyes and mouth told her he was exhausted, and rightly so after all he'd been through and suffered.

He woke up when they stopped long enough for her to walk the horses and clean their stalls. After she fixed him snacks, he went back to sleep and they were once again underway. The weather was cooperating. Cold, but no snowstorms. It made for easy driving for her.

The hard part of this journey home was his question, and it had been torturing her all day. *What else would stand in the way of your accepting my offer?*

Liz had one simple answer.

Reva.

Sadie had come right out and said it to Liz's face, *in front of Jarod,* that Reva still had a stranglehold on him. Jarod hadn't denied it. No one knew Connor better than his brother, so Liz knew what her answer would have to be.

Connor had a cowboy's heart.

There'd been a million songs written about the one woman a cowboy couldn't forget. It was the way a cowboy was put together. You couldn't fight it.

She'd wanted to see inside the cover. Now that the inside was exposed, it was time for her to move on. Her life depended on it.

After they'd parked for the night, she went into the trailer and pulled out the sofa bed so he could lie down. Once she'd made him comfortable and fed him, she checked on the horses and cleaned the stalls. With that task out of the way, she showered and put on her pajamas.

Flipping off the light switch, she used the ladder to reach the niche. But now the tables were turned, because she was exhausted and he was wide-awake, wanting to talk.

"You've had enough time to consider my offer. What's it going to be?"

She'd prepared her speech. "I'm honored that you have enough faith in me as a vet to help get your business off the ground, but I've thought it over and want to work on the reservation. Once you advertise, you'll find a great vet anxious to work with someone of your reputation. But not every vet wants to live on a reservation.

"I love it there and would like to think I could make

a meaningful contribution. The Crow love their animals and understand things about them I'd like to learn. Between my work there and at the clinic, I know I'm going to find fulfillment now that my barrel-racing days are over."

"In that case, before you go to sleep, there's something I couldn't give you in front of the others. If you'd come down for just a minute."

"It can't wait until morning?"

"I'm afraid not."

Puzzled, she threw off the covers and lowered herself to the floor.

"Come over here."

"I can hardly see you." She made her way to the side of his bed. He reached for her with his good arm and pulled her down next to him.

"Hold out your hand."

When Liz did his bidding, she heard a tinkling before he put the charm bracelet in her palm. She let out a cry of surprise. "What are you doing?"

"Since I can't do it myself, I need you to put it on your wrist for me."

"But Ralph gave this to both of us to keep in your cab for luck—"

"This bracelet *is* ours, and it did bring us luck, but instead of keeping it on the mirror, I want you to wear it. Put it on, please."

Liz felt all jittery. It took her forever to fasten it. "Okay. It's done."

She felt his hand circle her wrist and feel for the individual charms. "Ah. There it is. I've found the heart. Grandpa said it meant love of country, but between you and me it represents *my* heart."

A strangely warm shiver passed through her body.

"I lost it to you on the drive to Las Vegas. It happened that first magical night, while we were outside in the snow with our children wondering if they were enamored. Remember?"

"Yes." Her voice shook. "How could I ever forget one second of our time together?"

"That's when I realized I was enamored of *you*. The fact is, I'm so terribly in love with you, I can't take another step without you. Wear this instead of an engagement ring until I can buy you one. If I thought you didn't love me back, I'd never get over it. You do love me, don't you?"

That trace of vulnerability in his voice got to her every time. "Oh, Connor—"

"Oh, Connor, yes? Or no?"

"You *know* I do. I love you more than life itself and have done from a distance since the time I was a teenager."

"Now she tells me." He let out a yelp of happiness.

She tried to breathe, but he was squeezing her with his good arm. "When you asked me to drive to Las Vegas with you, I thought I'd die for joy and leaped at the chance to be with you, even knowing about Reva."

"I wanted you to drive with me and resorted to my first lie so you wouldn't refuse me. Yes, I married Reva, but that was a time of life when I didn't know who I was. Neither did she. It was a marriage that never took. Without substance, the physical side of it eventually fizzled. She's my past. *You're* my future, Liz Henson. Tell me you'll marry me, or I won't be able to handle it."

"I can't believe this is happening."

"Say it," he begged.

"Of course I'll marry you!"

"And be my vet?"

She laughed. "Yes."

"And be the mother of our children?"

The tears had started. "Yes."

"And love me forever, the way I love you?"

"Oh, yes, darling, yes, yes, yes!" Her whole soul was crying for joy.

"Thank God. Lie down next to me. I need to feel your beautiful body against me. The night you came up to the niche and we ate the Snickers together, I wanted you so badly it terrified me."

"I wanted you, too. Way too much." Her voice trembled.

"You're so beautiful, Liz. You have no idea." He'd said those words to her in the hospital. It hadn't been the drugs after all. "Come closer, sweetheart."

"I'm afraid I'll hurt your arm."

"You're the doc and know how to be careful. I'll let you handle me. You're the only one who can. But be warned that one day soon it'll be my turn. For right now, just kiss me the way you kissed me in the pool. You lit a fire in me that's never going to burn out. I love you and can't wait to make you my wife."

With those words he transformed her world. "There's nothing I want more," she whispered against his lips after devouring him. "Do you have any idea how much fun it is to do what I want to you?"

"Yup. Just keep it up."

Breathless and eager to accommodate him, she kept it up until the fire was blazing hot. "I—I'd better leave you alone," she stammered, realizing she wasn't being careful enough.

"Don't you dare move! Until we get married, and maybe for several months after, will you live with me in my trailer?"

"I'm so glad you said that," she cried into his neck. "It felt like home to me the minute we left my parents' house. I've never known the kind of happiness I've had with you, Connor."

In his hunger, he leaned over to kiss her again, forgetting about his handicap. "Ouch—this arm." He had to lie back.

She chuckled in spite of the desire raging through her body. "That arm won you five gold buckles. Just be patient, and in six weeks all your body parts will be working again in perfect harmony."

"I have news for you, sweetheart. They're all working right now."

"I know. I've got the same problem, so I think it will be better if I just hold you for what's left of the rest of this night."

"Promise you won't leave me?"

"What do you think?"

"I think I'm the luckiest man alive."

AT NINE-THIRTY THE next night Liz pulled up in front of the Bannock ranch house. For once, they were putting Ralph before the horses they needed to put into their barns. They wanted to surprise him. The others wouldn't be home until tomorrow.

When she looked over at Connor, she saw such a different man than the one she'd left with two and a half weeks ago, she hardly recognized him.

The lines and shadows of self-doubt, guilt and re-crimination were gone. If you could ascribe such an expression to a man, his striking face beamed with excitement. "Let's go break the news to him, sweetheart."

"I'll grab one each of our gold buckles to give him for a souvenir."

His brown eyes glowed as he looked at her. "Trust you to know what will touch his heart more than anything."

"Your coming home safe and sound will be the answer to his prayers. These trinkets are just the icing on the proverbial cake." She leaned across to kiss him long and hard before alighting from the cab.

Montana had been visited with more snow, creating another fairyland. After she'd gone into the trailer for the boxes, Connor wrapped his good arm around her waist and they walked up to the porch. He kissed her again. "Remember being here?"

"As if I could forget."

"It seemed so right that you and I were going off together to do what we loved."

"I thought the same thing."

"It was meant to be."

"Yes, darling."

He unlocked the door and they went inside. They crept down the hall to the den, but it was dark. "He's gone to bed."

"Maybe we should come back in the morning."

Connor shook his head. "No…this news can't wait." As he grasped her hand, the housekeeper approached.

"You're home! I'm so sorry about your arm. You would have won the whole thing, Connor. Congratulations to both of you!"

"Thank you," they said before he kissed her cheek.

"He's going to be so thrilled, you can't imagine!"

"We're the ones who are thrilled." He grasped Liz's hand and led her all the way back to Ralph's bedroom. They found him lying propped up in bed. He was reading a book by the light of the bedside table.

"Grandpa?"

Ralph looked up. The book fell out of his hand. "It's you. You're home!"

"I am. I brought someone with me."

He pulled Liz into the room with him. While Ralph stared at the two of them, they walked over to the side of his bed.

"We have some gifts for you." Liz handed him the two boxes, which he opened. "Those are yours to keep. You always had faith in us."

Tears spilled down his cheeks. "I heard your speech at the hotel. I've been crying ever since."

"We've got something else to tell you that'll make you cry even harder. Show him, sweetheart." She tugged on the sleeve of her pullover so Ralph could see the charm bracelet. "I've asked Liz to marry me."

His grandfather gasped.

"We made it official last night with this bracelet you gave us. It brought us luck and love. The kind you had with Grandma. It's the kind of love I've wanted with every fiber of my being. I know I've found it with Liz."

Ralph's eyes shone. "I know you have, too. My little princess. I always wanted you for my Connor. My dream has finally come true."

"I've loved him forever." Her words came out sounding like a croak.

"Come here and let me give both of you a hug."

After he let them go, he said, "Who else knows?"

Connor's eyes danced. "No one. You're the first. We'll tell everyone tomorrow when they're back."

"What are your plans?"

"We want to be married at Liz's church, but that's as far as we've gotten. We want it to be soon."

"Where will you live?"

"Here on the ranch. Until we build our own home, we'll live in my trailer."

A big smile broke out on his face. "You've brought me such wonderful news, I might expire from too much joy."

"Oh, please don't do that," Liz cried. "We're planning on you living a long time.

"We want our children to enjoy their great-grandfather for as long as possible. But now we're going to say good-night. We have to take care of our other children."

Ralph chuckled. "Your horses did themselves proud."

Connor nodded. "Especially Polly. She pulled through like a champion."

"I told her she had to do it for Connor, who couldn't compete for himself. I'm positive she understood me."

Ralph winked at her. "You've always had special powers in that department."

Liz watched Connor give his grandfather another kiss. "We'll come in the morning and have breakfast with you."

"Can't wait. We'll watch all the recordings and you can tell me everything that was going on behind the scenes. Especially the moment when that hooky honker pulled that stunt on you, son."

"He was a rank one, all right. Sleep well," Connor said, before ushering Liz out of the bedroom.

"What do you say we stall both horses in our barn for tonight? We'll put Sunflower next to Firebrand so they'll be happy."

"I was just going to suggest it. Who knows? Maybe they're engaged, too."

He threw back his head and laughed that deep, rich male laughter she loved almost as much as she loved him.

Once the horses were safely housed in the barn, Connor told her where to park his rig for the night. He helped her clean out the trailer stalls the best he could until they were able to go to bed themselves.

After showering, she cuddled up to Connor's solid, hard body. Talk about heaven. He only put on the bottom half of his sweats. It was too hard to deal with the top. "Darling? I've never seen Ralph so happy."

"Our news did it, all right. Can you imagine how happy everyone else is going to be when they hear?"

"My parents will be overjoyed."

"So will the rest of my family. Now they won't have to worry about me anymore."

"Mine won't, either. When I told Mom I was driving with you, she almost had a heart attack for fear I'd be hurt. That was because she knew Sadie and I had always been pining for love of the Bannock brothers."

"Unfortunately, the Bannock brothers had been warned off your land. I hope lightning won't strike me if I say Daniel Corkin's passing was a good thing. He put me and my brother through hell."

"Speaking of Jarod, do you want hear something kind of spooky?"

He plundered her mouth for a little while before he said, "I'm all ears."

"The first night I called Sadie from Las Vegas, she told me I was going to win because Jarod had seen a vision. When I asked if he'd had one about you winning, he said no."

"He's a lot like his uncle Charlo. I'm glad you didn't tell me, sweetheart."

She shivered. "I wonder why he told Sadie."

"They share everything. He probably told her not to tell you. But she did anyway, because she loves you and wanted to instill you with extra confidence."

"I'm afraid it did the opposite. For the rest of the time, all I did was worry about you. When Derrick told me you'd had an accident, it was like a nightmare come true. How specific are Jarod's visions?"

"Let's ask him tomorrow."

"Maybe we'd better not, or we might get Sadie into trouble."

"Don't worry about it. He loves her too much. I'm more inclined to believe he knew she'd tell you. Jarod wanted you to believe in yourself."

She cupped his face in her hands, kissing every feature. "With everyone believing in me, especially you, how could I lose? I fall more in love with you every minute. I wish—"

"So do I." His voice had grown husky. "Do me a favor and help me to love you any way we can until I can get rid of this sling."

"Well, as long as I've got your permission…"

"You've got it, Mrs. Bannock to be. In spades."

* * * * *

Watch for the next story in Rebecca Winters'
HITTING ROCKS COWBOYS *miniseries,*
THE NEW COWBOY,
coming soon from Harlequin American Romance!

#1509 HER FOREVER COWBOY
Forever, Texas
by Marie Ferrarella
Leaving her city life—and a bad fiancé—behind,
Dr. Alisha Cordell shows up in Forever, Texas. The move
is temporary...that is until she meets Brett Murphy, a charming
cowboy who has every intention of convincing her to stay!

#1514 THE TEXAN'S TWINS
Texas Rodeo Barons
by Pamela Britton
Rodeo cowboy Jet Baron can't stop thinking about
Jasmine Marks. But when he learns she's a single mom of
twin girls, he thinks he might be in over his head!

#1515 THE SURPRISE TRIPLETS
Safe Harbor Medical
by Jacqueline Diamond
Melissa and Edmond's marriage ended because he didn't
want children. Years later, he is appointed the guardian to his
seven-year-old niece and needs his ex's help—only to find
Melissa's pregnant...with triplets!

#1516 COWBOY IN THE MAKING
by Julie Benson
While recovering from an injury on his grandfather's ranch,
city boy Jamie Westland is drawn to Emma Donovan. But can
this wannabe cowboy find happiness with a country gal?

REQUEST YOUR FREE BOOKS!
2 FREE NOVELS PLUS 2 FREE GIFTS!

☘ HARLEQUIN®

American ★ Romance®

LOVE, HOME & HAPPINESS

YES! Please send me 2 FREE Harlequin® American Romance® novels and my 2 FREE gifts (gifts are worth about $10). After receiving them, if I don't wish to receive any more books, I can return the shipping statement marked "cancel." If I don't cancel, I will receive 4 brand-new novels every month and be billed just $4.74 per book in the U.S. or $5.24 per book in Canada. That's a savings of at least 14% off the cover price! It's quite a bargain! Shipping and handling is just 50¢ per book in the U.S. and 75¢ per book in Canada.* I understand that accepting the 2 free books and gifts places me under no obligation to buy anything. I can always return a shipment and cancel at any time. Even if I never buy another book, the two free books and gifts are mine to keep forever.

154/354 HDN F4YN

Name _____ (PLEASE PRINT) _____

Address _____ Apt. #

City _____ State/Prov. _____ Zip/Postal Code

Signature (if under 18, a parent or guardian must sign)

Mail to the Harlequin® Reader Service:
IN U.S.A.: P.O. Box 1867, Buffalo, NY 14240-1867
IN CANADA: P.O. Box 609, Fort Erie, Ontario L2A 5X3

Want to try two free books from another line?
Call 1-800-873-8635 or visit www.ReaderService.com.

* Terms and prices subject to change without notice. Prices do not include applicable taxes. Sales tax applicable in N.Y. Canadian residents will be charged applicable taxes. Offer not valid in Quebec. This offer is limited to one order per household. Not valid for current subscribers to Harlequin American Romance books. All orders subject to credit approval. Credit or debit balances in a customer's account(s) may be offset by any other outstanding balance owed by or to the customer. Please allow 4 to 6 weeks for delivery. Offer available while quantities last.

Your Privacy—The Harlequin® Reader Service is committed to protecting your privacy. Our Privacy Policy is available online at www.ReaderService.com or upon request from the Harlequin Reader Service.

We make a portion of our mailing list available to reputable third parties that offer products we believe may interest you. If you prefer that we not exchange your name with third parties, or if you wish to clarify or modify your communication preferences, please visit us at www.ReaderService.com/consumerschoice or write to us at Harlequin Reader Service Preference Service, P.O. Box 9062, Buffalo, NY 14269. Include your complete name and address.

HAR13R

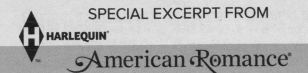
"You going to take off your dress now? Or later?"

The woman's eyes widened. *"Excuse me?"*

"Don't worry. My friends didn't know I was meeting a man. A project engineer, actually, and you don't exactly look the part. Nice try, though."

"Let me guess—Jet Baron."

"One and the same." He gave her a welcoming smile, his gaze slowly sliding over her body.

"Why am I *not* surprised?" she asked.

Her sarcasm startled him, as did the way she eyed him up and down. So direct. So appraising. So…disappointed.

He straightened. "If you're going to start stripping, you better do it now. I'm expecting the engineer at any moment."

"You think I'm some kind of prank. An actress hired to, what? Pretend to have a meeting with you? Then strip out of my clothes?"

He was starting to get a funny feeling. "Well, yeah."

She took a step toward him, and he would be lying if he didn't feel as if, somehow, the joke was on him.

"Tell me something, what makes you think the engineer in question is a man?"

"I was told that."

"By whom?"

"I don't know who told me, I just know he's a man. All engineers in the oil industry are men."

She took another step toward him. "There are actually quite a few women in the business. I graduated from Berkley with a degree in geology." She took yet another step closer. "I interned for the USGS out of Menlo Park then moved back to Texas to get my master's in engineering. My father was a wildcatter, and it was from him that I learned the business—so let me reassure you, Mr. Baron, I can tell the difference between an injection hose and a drill pipe. But if you still insist only men can be engineers, perhaps we should call your sister, Lizzie, who hired me."

Jet couldn't speak for a moment. "Oh, crap."

Her extraordinary blue eyes scanned him, her derision clearly evident. "Still want me to strip?"

He almost said yes, but he could tell that he was in enough trouble as it is. "I take it you're J.C.?"

"I am."

"I should apologize."

"You think?"

Look for THE TEXAN'S TWINS
by Pamela Britton next month from
Harlequin® American Romance®.

American Romance®

You Can't Hide in Forever

The minute he lays eyes on Forever's new doctor, Brett Murphy
knows the town—and he—won't be the same. Alisha Cordell is
raising the temperature of every male within miles. But the big-city
blonde isn't looking to put down roots. The saloon owner and
rancher will just have to change the reticent lady doc's mind.

A week after she caught her fiancé cheating, Alisha was on a train
headed for a Texas town that was barely a blip on the map.
So she's stunned at how fast the place is growing on her.
That includes the sexy cowboy with the sassy smile and easygoing
charm. Brett's also been burned by love, but he's eager for a second
chance…with Alisha. Is she ready to make Brett—and Forever—
part of her long-term plans?

Look for
Her Forever Cowboy
by *USA TODAY* bestselling author
MARIE FERRARELLA
from the **Forever, Texas** miniseries from
Harlequin® American Romance®.

Available September 2014
wherever books and ebooks are sold.

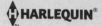
HARLEQUIN®

American Romance®

Triple the Trouble

When fertility counselor Melissa Everhart decided to have a baby on her own, she didn't anticipate triplets…or her ex-husband's return to Safe Harbor. Three years ago, Edmond's reluctance to have children tore them apart. But now that he's been made guardian of his niece, Melissa witnesses how tenderly he cares for the little girl.

Though Edmond doesn't believe he's father material, his sudden custody of Dawn leaves him little choice. He turns to Melissa, the warmest, kindest person he knows, for help. They begin to rediscover the love they once shared, but the betrayals of the past trouble them both. Can they find the forgiveness they both need to come together as a family?

Look for
The Surprise Triplets
by JACQUELINE DIAMOND
from the *Safe Harbor Medical* miniseries from
Harlequin® American Romance®.

**Available September 2014
wherever books and ebooks are sold.**

Also available from the *Safe Harbor Medical* miniseries
by Jacqueline Diamond:
A Baby for the Doctor
The Surprise Holiday Dad
His Baby Dream
The Baby Jackpot

www.Harlequin.com